DUSK

Dusk shares her life with hawks not people.

People are enemies.

She should hate Boy.

But her human heart is telling her something different . . .

DUSK

SUSAN GATES

PUFFIN

PUFFIN BOOKS

Published by the Penguin Group
Penguin Books Ltd, 80 Strand, London WC2R 0RL, England
Penguin Group (USA), Inc., 375 Hudson Street, New York, New York 10014, USA
Penguin Books Australia Ltd, 250 Camberwell Road, Camberwell, Victoria 3124, Australia
Penguin Books Canada Ltd, 10 Alcorn Avenue, Toronto, Ontario, Canada M4V 3B2
Penguin Books India (P) Ltd, 11 Community Centre, Panchsheel Park, New Delhi – 110 017, India
Penguin Books (NZ) Ltd, Cnr Rosedale and Airborne Roads, Albany, Auckland, New Zealand
Penguin Books (South Africa) (Pty) Ltd, 24 Sturdee Avenue, Rosebank 2196, South Africa

Penguin Books Ltd, Registered Offices: 80 Strand, London WC2R 0RL, England

www.penguin.com

First published 2004
1

Set in 11/15.25 pt Adobe Sabon
Typeset by Rowland Phototypesetting Ltd, Bury St Edmunds, Suffolk

Made and printed in England by Clays Ltd, St Ives plc

British Library Cataloguing in Publication Data
A CIP catalogue record for this book is available from the British Library

ISBN 0-141-31705-1

1

'You never give me any trouble do you, General?' said the lab assistant, stripping off his thick, protective gloves.

He was cleaning out the rats. He hated that job. Those rats were psycho. They'd rip you to shreds if they got half the chance. The only one that wasn't crazy was the big, white one, in the cage at the end. The other lab rats had numbers. But the lab assistants had a name for the white one. They called him 'General Rat'.

The General never tried to attack you. But he spooked you somehow. He was much bigger than the other rats. Bred so his head had extra brain space. He was smarter too, so the scientists said. He was a super-smart rat who could work things out. There was a big, shaved patch on his head and a silver plate screwed into his skull that made him look half rat, half robot.

'You're probably smarter than me, boy,' grinned the lab assistant at the General, not for a second suspecting it might be true. 'And they say you're going to live a long time. That your body just won't wear out. It's amazing what these guys can do. But what have you got to look forward to, eh? More electrodes stuck inside your brain?'

The General watched quietly from his cage. The other rats were too dumb to notice. They'd been bred for aggression and nothing else. And the experiment had been a great success – they were vicious as piranhas. But the General had been bred to have brainpower. He'd already noticed that this lab assistant was a sloppy worker. That he made mistakes, broke safety procedures. He hadn't put the metal clips back on the rats' cages. He should have done that straightaway. The General was thinking about the best way to take advantage of that.

The lab assistant shivered. The General's red eyes seemed to pierce through to your soul, search out your every weakness.

The lab assistant had only been here a few months. He was pleased to get the job. There wasn't much employment up here, in the backwoods. But the things they did at this military research establishment gave him the creeps. They'd do anything to engineer the perfect soldier. You need him smarter, more violent, with better night vision? No problem!

What was behind the locked door was part of those experiments. The door was at the end of the lab. NO UNAUTHORIZED PERSONNEL, said the sign on it. STRICTLY OFF LIMITS TO ALL CIVILIANS.

But the lab assistant had seen and heard things when he was supposed to be attending to his rat cleaning duties. He'd seen scientists going in and out, heard the angry shrieks and cries of a wild animal.

Some kind of primate? wondered the lab assistant. But this was the kind of place where it was best not to notice too much. You just did your job, kept your head down and went home. The army didn't like people who asked questions, poked their noses into army business.

Then he saw them thawing out dead mice in the microwave. They took the soggy defrosted bodies inside the room.

'Dinner time, Dusk,' he heard somebody say. The cries became shrill, excited. Whatever was in there liked to eat mice. It had a name. And it spent most of its life drugged, in a sleepy trance. Before the scientists took mice in, they hid pills inside them, shoved them down their gullets. The lab assistant had taken a sneaky look at the pill bottle. They were sedatives.

But whatever was in there, it wasn't his business to know about it.

He took the stopper out of a bottle of pure alcohol, started swabbing down the bench surfaces. He needn't have hurried. He was alone in the lab – something that had never happened before. The scientists were in a big meeting with some top brass military men.

But someone was still checking up on him. It was the General, tracking his every move.

What are you doing, you idiot? the lab assistant scolded himself. He was making stupid mistakes – again. He smacked his forehead in frustration. That was a bad idea; it just made his headache worse. *How many beers did you have last night? You still haven't put them clips back on!* If he wasn't careful, drink would lose him this job. Just like it had lost him all the others.

He hurried back to the rat cages.

'Hungry!' came a shriek from behind the forbidden door.

The lab assistant stopped dead. He thought his ears were playing tricks. Then more shrieks came, shrill and angry.

'Dinner! Now!'

'It can talk,' whispered the lab assistant. 'What the hell is it?'

He checked the corridor. The meeting room door was still closed. They'd be in there until lunchtime. No one else was about. He hurried back into the lab.

Shall I? he thought, looking at the locked door. He'd be in big trouble if he got found out. But his job was already on the line. He'd been given two formal warnings for ignoring safety procedures. He'd never been any good at following rules.

Wouldn't mind knowing some of these army bastards' secrets, he thought.

It felt like his own little mutiny, before they sacked him. Besides, he was curious. What kind of creature had they got shut up in there?

He knew where to get the keys. The Chief Scientist had a tiny office, just a cubbyhole off the lab. He'd left the keys in the left-hand drawer of his desk.

The lab assistant shook his head. He wasn't the only one who was sloppy about security. But he got it in the neck, while his bosses never got blamed.

He walked towards the locked door, hesitated. His hands were shaking and it wasn't just because of last night's hard drinking.

If you're gonna do it, Curtis, he urged himself, *be quick!*

Behind him the rats were doing their usual thing. Hurling themselves at the bars of their cages, gnawing the metal. Only today they seemed even more hyper than usual.

What's wrong with them? thought Curtis, as he stood, dithering, before the door.

Only General Rat didn't freak out. He was observing Curtis like the scientists observed him. His brain was sharp and clear. The humans who engineered him knew he was smarter than your average rat. They thought he was maybe dog smart, even dolphin smart. What they hadn't considered was that a really smart rat can deliberately flunk his intelligence tests. Give himself a lower score. Although they didn't know it, the General was human smart. And like humans, he had ambitions, plans, a desire for power.

Curtis was psyching himself up. *I won't get another chance*, he told himself. It felt good going behind the back of the Chief Scientist. *Pompous creep*, thought Curtis. He'd only ever spoken to Curtis twice. And both times Curtis had felt patronized. But all local, civilian workers were treated like that at SERU. That was the official name of this place. SERU – Sensory Enhancement Research Unit.

Curtis selected a key from the bunch. Tried it in the door. Wrong choice. He selected another one. The third one fitted.

He walked into the room. It was another lab, with

computers, scientific equipment, all the usual stuff. There were three computer disks, just left out on a bench.

Careless, thought Curtis. They obviously thought this lab was secure. Weren't expecting anyone like him to sneak in. He slid one of the disks into his jeans pocket as he passed. He might learn something from it later.

Then he saw what he was looking for. A cage, built into an alcove, further down the room.

Curtis couldn't see what was in it. He went closer, cautiously. It was a big cage. Those cries of rage he'd heard – anything that screeched like that had to be dangerous. They wouldn't have to drug it up if it wasn't. But it was quiet now. Curtis peered though the bars.

'It's a girl!'

She was slumped zombie-like, in one corner of the cage. She looked like any normal kid, in shorts, T-shirt, scruffy unlaced trainers. She had a shaggy mane of white-blonde hair.

What they got her shut up like this for? thought Curtis, shocked. He had a son, Jay. Jay would go crazy if he was locked up like this.

Then he noticed her arms. They were criss-crossed with scratches. Some were old, scabbed over. Some were fresh, still bleeding. Did she do that to herself?

'Hey!' he called softly to her. 'Hey, little girl.'

Dusk's eyes shot open. They were brilliant orange. Their vivid glare was so wild, so savage that Curtis staggered back.

Is she human? he thought. He'd never seen eyes like that before, not in humans.

Dusk shook her head like a dog, as she always did, trying to get rid of that groggy feeling. It never went entirely.

The scientists said, 'It's for her own good.' It kept her manageable, made her sleep a lot. Even when she was awake, Dusk felt dozy, unconnected, as if there was cloudy glass between herself and the rest of the world. Except when she was self harming. It was the only power she had, to hurt herself. And it was only when she felt the pain that Dusk knew she was alive.

She stumbled to the bars. To Dusk, Curtis was just another person in a white coat. The rota of people who fed her changed constantly. There was never any chance of forming a relationship. As with the other lab animals, her carers were warned against it. 'Stick to the routine. Strictly no stimulation. Let her drift through the days.' It made it easier for everyone.

None of them guessed how, when Dusk wasn't too drugged up, she watched them, picking up words, behaviour, learning all the time. There was much more going on inside her head than they realized, or wanted to acknowledge.

'Want dinner!' demanded Dusk. Her empty belly told her it was way past feeding time.

She got frantic when she was kept waiting. She thought she might never be fed again. She shrieked, angrily.

'Shush!' said Curtis, putting his finger to his lips. He was struggling to cope with the shock. Still staring at those startling orange eyes that told you she wasn't one hundred per cent human.

What is she? he thought. *Some kind of mutant?* What

had those army ghouls been up to? No wonder they'd kept her locked away. She was about Jay's age, maybe eleven years old, far as he could tell . . .

Dusk rattled the bars. *Why was he standing there? Why wasn't he bringing food?* She began whimpering. She didn't sound like a wild animal now, but a scared little girl.

Helpless to make food come, she clawed at her arms, opening old scabs, making herself bleed.

'Don't do that!' said Curtis, horrified.

He tried to think of a way of distracting her. *What do little girls like?* He had no idea. He didn't have a daughter. Only Jay. But he didn't know what he liked either.

Feverishly, he searched in his lab coat pockets. They were full of useless junk. He hadn't cleaned them out since he started here. Right at the bottom he found something. He'd got it in a cracker at the Christmas party, with a joke and a paper hat. He blew the fluff off it, rubbed it on his cuff until it shone.

'Here.' He tried to keep his voice kind and coaxing. As you would to a timid animal you don't want to panic.

He held it out to her. It was a cheap trashy hair slide, made of blue plastic, with fake glass diamonds that sparkled.

'Here. Take it.'

Dusk stopped hurting herself. She glared at Curtis, suspiciously.

Curtis thought, *What have those army bastards done to her?*

When he spoke next, he couldn't keep the pity out of his voice. 'Do you like it, Dusk?' He shook the hair slide.

Immediately her orange eyes locked on to it. They still had that glazed-over, unfocused look. But her last dose of sedative was wearing off. The world around her didn't look quite so foggy. She followed the glitter of the fake glass diamonds, fascinated. She gave shrill shrieks like an excited child.

She likes it, thought Curtis. He told her, 'It's yours. It's a present.' He had no idea if she understood. But a blood-streaked arm shot out the cage, snatched the hair slide.

Then tried to cram it into her mouth.

'No,' said Curtis. 'No, Dusk. It's for putting in your hair.'

He mimed the actions. Pretended to push a slide into his own thinning hair. He said, 'It's for keeping your hair tidy.'

Dusk didn't seem to be listening. She had the hair slide clutched in her fist. She opened her fingers one by one, hypnotized by its sparkle.

Then, to Curtis's surprise, she copied him, tried to jam the slide into her hair. It wouldn't go in; her hair was too tangled.

'Here, here,' said Curtis, searching in his pocket again. 'Comb your hair first.'

Dusk's hair got combed, now and again. But they did it when she was sedated or else she fought like a tiger. She'd never done it for herself. She stared, bewildered, at the comb.

'You do this,' said Curtis, raking it through his own hair. He wiped off the grease and dandruff, handed it to her through the bars. Dusk shrank back, didn't take it. He dropped it on the floor of her cage. She snatched it up. She copied Curtis again, tugging the comb through her hair.

'Gently,' said Curtis. She didn't understand. He put both his hands out, palms down, patted the air, in a calming gesture. 'Gently.' Those cruel orange eyes watched his every move. She seemed to get the message.

Dusk stopped trying to drag the comb through. Slid it over her hair. It didn't get the tangles out, but the rhythmic action seemed to soothe her. She didn't smile. Her face was almost comically serious, like a little child's concentrating hard on getting something right. For a few minutes it was peaceful in the lab. No shrieks, or rattling of cage bars. The only sound was the background hum of the computers.

Curtis thought, *Is this really happening?* He was standing in a top-secret lab watching some poor little orange-eyed freak comb her hair. It was more surreal than any of his drunken dreams.

Dusk stopped combing, jammed in the hair slide. Managed to click it shut.

'That's good,' Curtis heard himself say. 'You know what? You're clever, Dusk. And you look real pretty.'

He reached through the bars to pat her hand. He didn't know why he did it – just to make human contact, give her some kind of comfort.

It was the wrong move.

Dusk shrieked. She flung the comb away. She hated being touched. That wild look came back into her eyes.

I've blown it, thought Curtis.

She hissed at him like a snake. Then spat in his face. And Curtis knew for sure she wasn't even close to being normal. Or maybe even close to being human.

'Quit that!' said Curtis, wiping his face with his sleeve. 'Why'd you do that?'

'Dinner!' she demanded.

Curtis thought, stupidly, *Does she mean mice?* He'd seen scientists taking them in. Could they really have been for her?

He frowned, unsure what to do. Best to lock the door, walk away, forget he'd ever been in here.

But just as he'd decided to do that, Dusk went manic, ripping at her flesh, screeching, spitting, bouncing off the bars like a zoo animal gone crazy.

'Shush!' begged Curtis. He wished he'd never come in here. He should have minded his own business. They were going to hear her all over the building.

'I'll feed you. I'll feed you. Right? Just shut up!' said Curtis frantically. Did she understand? He didn't have time to find out.

He raced back to the storeroom. Yanked open the freezer. Curtis didn't even put on gloves – Dusk was still screeching. He just smashed the edge off a block of ice. Mice were frozen inside it. You could see their tails, pink ears, eyes like black beads. Curtis stuck them in the microwave to defrost them.

Ping.

In the other lab Dusk heard the ping. She knew food was coming. Her cries changed. They were shrill now, excited.

11

Curtis came running out of the storeroom. His hands were shaking so badly he could hardly hold the slippery mouse bodies. He expected his bosses to come running in any minute and yell at him, 'What's going on here?'

While Curtis was rushing about like a headless chicken, General Rat had seen his chance. He was squeezing out of his cage. It was easy. He just climbed up the wire netting, nudged up the lid that Curtis had left unclipped and slithered to freedom.

Curtis didn't notice. He was far too preoccupied, trying to make that screaming freak shut up.

As Curtis hurried past the bench, the sleeve of his lab coat caught the bottle of alcohol. He hadn't put the stopper back in. Just another safety rule he'd broken.

Horrified, he saw it topple, tried to grab it. His reactions were way too slow. Alcohol flowed over the bench top. The bottle rolled into the sink.

Damn! thought Curtis. Had he turned off that Bunsen burner? He squinted further down the bench. Was that a tiny blue flame flickering? He couldn't tell.

He thought he still had time. He didn't know the bench top was already alight. That the alcohol had instantly ignited. But that its flames were invisible to human eyes.

Dusk could see the flames though, through the open door. Even from her cage right at the end of the other lab. She had highly specialized vision. She could see the tiniest flicker of light, movement, shadow.

She started screeching alarm calls.

Curtis dived for the burner. As he reached across the bench, his lab coat caught fire. This time even he could see it. Orange flames licked round his cuff, raced up his sleeve.

Terrified now, Curtis ripped off his lab coat, his arms flailing wildly. A whole rack of alcohol bottles crashed to the floor.

Instantly the floor burst alight like a fiery sea. His trainers caught fire. He could smell rubber burning. He thought, *Get out of here!* Then one of Dusk's shrieks ripped through the air.

Curtis cursed himself. 'Just run, you stupid bastard.'

He told himself, *I've been a coward all my life. What difference will one more time make? She ain't even human.* But he thought of her cries of delight at the hair slide. And he knew he couldn't leave her. Not to burn alive. What kind of monster would do that?

Behind him, the plastic-coated bench tops were melting. Thick, oily smoke curled up to the fire alarms. They started wailing out warnings. The flames flowed out into the corridor, under the meeting room door.

The military men and scientists in the meeting room were getting up out of their chairs. They didn't rush.

Someone said, 'It's probably just a fire drill. They have them all the time.' But then someone's shoe caught alight.

It took a few seconds for them to realize they were trapped. Then there were shouts, the sound of glass shattering as they smashed windows in a mad scramble to escape. The fire had plenty to feed on in the office. As it roared through the piles of papers and books it became an inferno.

13

Dusk huddled in the corner of her cage, screeching. Her orange eyes flashed with anger and fear. She could smell the stink of the smoke. Feel the flames' searing heat. Soon they would flow into this lab, run along the floor, shelves, set the ceiling alight.

She grabbed the cage bars to rattle them, screamed out in pain. They were already too hot to touch. She curled up, coughing, on the floor. Smoky flecks from the fire stung her eyes. Automatically, Dusk's third eyelids, semi-transparent membranes that protected her vision, slid across.

Curtis came out of the smoke. He had his protective gloves on, the ones he used for rat cleaning, and the keys he'd stolen from the Chief Scientist's office.

He fumbled with keys in the cage door. The thick gloves made him extra clumsy. He found the right one. It turned. He thought, *Why isn't the door opening?* Then he saw a bolt at the top, slid it back.

He yanked open the door, raced in and grabbed Dusk off the floor. 'Come on!' He knew they only had minutes before the fire engulfed this lab too.

Dusk fought, tried to rake out his eyes, but Curtis was too strong. He dragged her, kicking and screaming, to the Fire Door, pushed up the bar and bundled her outside. A hot blast of air shot out after them. Curtis couldn't keep hold of Dusk. He dumped her on the grass beside him, while he lay flapping on the ground, gasping for breath.

Back in the burning lab, the General barely had time to save his own skin. But he had to do something first. He needed an army. The General had plans.

14

He streaked through the smoke and flames like a white ghost. His fur was scorched. Glass flasks, heated white-hot, exploded all around him.

Some of his fellow captives had already escaped. Most were biting their bars in a fury, too stupid to know they were free. Even the free ones weren't running. They were too busy fighting, trying to kill each other. That's what they'd been bred for.

The General knew he had to take control quickly. He stood up on his back legs. The silver plate in his skull dazzled them. His red eyes blazed with command.

He squeaked, several short, sharp squeaks. Some carried on fighting. Some turned to look. He was bigger than they were, much stronger and much, much smarter. They crowded round him, squeaking. Rats like to follow a leader. And they had found their Chief.

Most followed him to safety through a ventilation grill. The General didn't hang around to wait for the others. He left them to burn alive. He had all the soldiers he needed – for starters.

Curtis was still sprawled on the grass. Boots thudded past him. Dazed, he raised his head. It was mayhem. Soldiers and civilians were running everywhere, some burning, hysterical, some shouting orders.

He thought, *Where's Dusk?* But then he started hurting. Curtis hadn't realized how badly he was burned. He sat up and rocked himself to and fro, locked in his own little pain-filled world.

Dusk sat up, saw Curtis rocking in distress. She did that too, sometimes, in her cage. To and fro, to and fro, trying to make herself feel better when longings she didn't understand, for tenderness, for some kind of loving contact, overwhelmed her.

Curtis looked up, saw Dusk through waves of pain. Saw her fierce eyes soften, saw her reach out a skinny arm, almost as if she wanted to comfort him. He stared at her, amazed.

But then someone staggered into her. She screeched in protest, snatched her arm back, sprang to her feet.

'Dusk!' shouted Curtis helplessly. He tried to get to his feet, couldn't and collapsed back on the ground.

Next second, Dusk was caught up in a whirlwind of people, whisked away from him.

'Hey!' someone shouted. 'There's a guy needs medical attention here!'

In the chaos, no one noticed the lab rats sweep past, with the General leading the way. Where were they heading? Only the General knew.

No one noticed, either, a wild-looking child, about eleven years old, heading for the main gate.

Dusk could see a way to freedom. There was a high electric fence all round the station. But the big security gates stood wide open to let the people and vehicles through. She could see the forest beyond. She shrank back, scared. All her life she'd had things done to her, been told what to do by people in white coats. She took a few, tentative steps forwards.

Then heard a deep, rumbling growl behind her. She almost wet herself.

'Wolf!'

Once, only once in her life, she'd made a bid for freedom. Broken away from her minders as she was being taken from lab to lab, burst through doors into the sunshine. She'd seen the forest then, for the first time, outside the fence, felt grass under her feet. But then she'd seen the guard dog, in his tiny pen built on to the side of the lab. He'd snarled at her, showed his white teeth.

People in white coats came rushing out to get her. 'Let's take you home,' one said. But they didn't need to persuade her. She'd raced ahead of them, back to the security of her cage and crouched in a corner, trembling. 'Don't run away again,' someone said, 'or Wolf will get you.'

Someone else said, 'Don't say that. You'll scare her.'

'She doesn't understand,' shrugged the person who'd made the threat. 'She's not even human.'

But Dusk understood much more than they ever imagined.

Dusk turned round, very slowly, her eyes fixed on Wolf. She couldn't run. She was frozen with fear. She could feel her heart fluttering in her chest like a trapped bird.

But Wolf wasn't snarling. He was quiet now. Even though he could smell the smoke, hear the screaming people. Dusk stared into his eyes, through the bars. For a killer dog, those eyes were surprisingly wise and calm. Dusk felt her heart slowing down.

People rushed past her, jostled her. But Dusk wasn't aware of them. Flames got nearer, raced along rooftops like fiery squirrels. Ashes from burning buildings swirled all around them. But it still didn't break their gaze. Dusk didn't think she was human – she'd heard them say so often enough at SERU. She wasn't sure what she was, where she belonged. But she saw something in Wolf's eyes she recognized.

Suddenly Dusk saw a picture in her head. She often thought in pictures. At SERU they'd taught her basic speech and she'd picked up more language just by listening. It was enough for her daily physical needs and for simple thoughts. But it didn't cover concepts, dreams, feelings.

Dusk pictured Wolf pacing in his cage. Then she made another picture in her mind. In this one Wolf was running free in the forest outside the fence. Where Dusk knew, just instinctively knew, there were no cages, no people in white coats.

His cage door was locked. But there was a little hatch where they shoved the meat in. That was only bolted. Dusk knew all about bolts. There was one on her cage door. She looked once more, deep into Wolf's eyes. Then, acting against all her instincts, slid back the bolt to let him out.

Straightaway Wolf nudged the hatch up with his nose. Pushed his head through. The rest of his body came wriggling after.

Dusk screeched alarm calls. She took off, horrified at what she'd just done. Dodged through shocked survivors staggering about, soldiers dragging fire hoses. She stood, shivering, by the main gates.

Before her, miles and miles of forest stretched to the horizon and beyond. She was scared of all that space.

She almost turned round, ran back to the burning lab. But the fire scared her too . . .

The fire made the sweat sheen on Curtis's face glow orange, then crimson. He half raised himself, on one elbow.

He thought he saw white-blonde hair, gleaming like a star, flying through the main gates.

Was it her? Could it be?

Anyway, it was gone now. Curtis slumped back, on to black crispy grass. He didn't want the military to find her, sedate her, shut her up again in that cage. But she needed taking care of. If that was her, if she had escaped, how was she going to survive out there, in the woods?

Poor little freak, he thought. *She never stood a chance.*

His eyes suddenly filled with tears. For all sorts of reasons – the shock, the pain, the way he'd failed his son, Jay, and the way he'd rescued, but then failed Dusk.

When the medical team finally reached him, they found Curtis crying helplessly, his body shaking with sobs.

2

Dusk had stopped running. Now she was wandering among trees in the woods that surrounded the research station. She was alone. No one had run this way. They were all heading for the nearest town, Prospect, a mile away down a dirt road.

Boom!

Back at SERU the fire had reached some gas canisters, stacked against an outside wall. Half the station went up in a giant fireball, including the lab where they'd kept Dusk. The squad of soldiers, sent in to rescue her, all died in the blast.

Dusk heard the explosion. But to her the noise sounded muffled and far away, from another world. It didn't concern her.

She thought, *Hungry.* She didn't know what to do about that. Dusk looked around, waiting for someone in a white coat to come and feed her. She was afraid. She thought, *Home.* She longed for the safety of her cage.

Dusk clawed compulsively at the scratches on her arm, opening old scabs, making them bleed.

Then she remembered something. She raked in her hair,

found the blue plastic hair slide. Rubbed it clean on her T-shirt, like Curtis did. Watched the fake diamonds sparkle. It comforted her somehow.

'Mine,' said Dusk defiantly, jamming it back into her hair.

No one had ever given Dusk a present. Curtis would have been amazed to know how much that cheap hair slide meant to her. How his clumsy attempt at kindness had rocked Dusk to the core. Thrown her ideas about people into confusion.

Other changes were taking place too, inside her head. It was hours since her last dose of sedative. Dusk was beginning to wake up. Lose that fuzzy, drugged-up feeling that, for so long, had kept her senses deadened. Like the kindness she'd had from Curtis, she'd never known what she was missing.

The world stood out sharp and clear, in all its complexity. The forest around her was a revelation.

Everywhere she looked was a swirling kaleidoscope of light, shadow, motion. At first, so much life dazzled her. She'd been brought up in the stark and sterile surroundings of scientific laboratories, with stimulation kept to the minimum. Now her senses were swamped.

Then, slowly, her orange eyes started to make sense of things. They zoomed in on the tremble of a grass stem. Saw a fly vibrating its shimmering wings. Each pollen grain seemed individual to her, each crumb of soil separate.

Everything excited her, as if she'd been born again – but this time fully alive. She pointed in wonder, like a baby, making fresh discoveries every second.

She took a step forwards. From springy pine needles into long grass. It swayed all around her, in a mist of yellow pollen. It tickled the back of her knees, made her laugh out loud. She was shocked by the new sound, coming from her own mouth. She'd never laughed before in her life. Her main emotions, when she was awake enough to feel anything at all, had been rage and panic.

What was that?

Her whole body quivered to attention. She saw movement, a flickering in the long grass. It was shady between the trees but that didn't matter. Dusk's eyes were designed to see in poor light. They'd been specially engineered for that.

'Food!' whispered Dusk, her body shivering in concentration. Food always excited her. At SERU food had been the high spot of her day. Her orange eyes gleamed fanatically.

Mice leave a trail. Their pee has a bright yellow glow. So have their droppings. Even the greasy sweat where they've rubbed against a grass stem. But it only shows up if you've got ultraviolet vision – like some predator insects do, or birds of prey.

Dusk could see it too, that giveaway golden gleam. Her eyes couldn't swivel in their sockets. So she swivelled her whole head instead.

A grass stalk shivered. *There!*

Dusk struck, quick as a snake, her hands out like talons. She missed the mouse. But it died of shock anyway. It never even knew what happened. Dusk picked it up, inspected its limp body. Then, dangling it by the tail, she dropped it into her mouth, gulped it down whole.

Dusk had caught her first prey. Done it all by herself.

All her life, things had been done to her. They'd fed her, given her clothes, walked her up and down labs on hard white tiles to get exercise. Every so often they performed experiments on her. They photographed her eyes, made her do tests. Now she'd found food for herself. She never knew she could do that.

Dusk grinned, thrilled by a sudden sense of her own power. A whole new world was opening up to her.

There! Dusk saw a shimmer in the grass.

Instinctively she pounced. This time it was a big fat beetle. She didn't have to be quick to catch it. It was just lumbering along, its wing covers gleaming in rainbow colours, like oil spilled on a road.

It didn't die of heart failure, like the mouse. But Dusk crammed it into her mouth and swallowed it, still kicking. She looked around for more, her orange eyes as precise as lasers . . .

A harsh mewing sound came from high above her. Dusk's head shot up, startled. Her eyes zoomed in. There was a bird of prey up there, circling among the clouds. Hovering on the thermals with stiff, outspread wings. Every second it seemed on the point of stalling, tumbling out of the sky. But it never did.

The bird cried again. Dusk called back to it, urgent, excited cries. Stretched up her arms as if she could reach it. Seeing it fly made her heart ache with longing, so intense it was like pain. She made a picture in her head.

23

She saw herself, up there with the hawk, soaring, drifting lazily. She could even feel warm air currents, cradling her body . . .

Dusk flapped her bony elbows, trying to fly after it, terrified she'd be left behind.

But the army scientists, tinkering with her embryo in a test tube, hadn't been interested in giving her wings. Their research brief was to clone eye genes from birds of prey and see if they would express themselves in humans. It was another step on the road to soldiers with perfect night vision.

The eye genes did express themselves. Dusk had hawk vision. But it was a big surprise when Dusk started showing other hawk characteristics. The scientists hadn't meant that to happen. From their point of view it made the experiment a failure.

Dusk flapped her arms again, desperate to join the hawk. She suddenly knew who she was, where she belonged . . .

Dusk heard a stick snapping, somewhere very close. She tore her eyes away from the hawk.

'Wolf!' she said.

You didn't need her super-sensitive eyes to see him. He wasn't trying to hide himself like the mouse. There was no predator in the woods that scared him. He came trotting through the trees as if he already had the sense of his own power that Dusk was only just discovering. But Dusk didn't feel powerful now. She was petrified, tried to scramble up a tree trunk. Instinctively, like a hawk, she wanted to be high up, with a bird's-eye view of the ground.

She'd chosen the wrong tree. It had smooth slippery bark that she couldn't cling to. She came sliding down again, screeching in panic. People in white coats usually came running when she did that, with food, or to top her up with sedatives. But no one came running now.

Dusk landed in a heap and instantly froze with terror. She could feel Wolf's hot breath on her neck. It stank of rotten meat. She swivelled her head round.

For a few seconds, one hunter's eyes stared into the eyes of another. Then Dusk bolted, ran like a hare, zigzagging between trees, leaping fallen branches.

Wolf watched her go. He could have caught her easily, with his long, loping stride. But he let her escape. He had other things on his mind. Wolf raised his head, ears perked. He heard faint barking in the distance. It came from Prospect, where there were lots of dogs. Some mangy strays, some pampered pooches. Wolf trotted on, following the sound. The first thing he meant to do was find himself a mate.

Dusk only stopped running when the trees ran out. She'd reached the edge of the forest.

She doubled up, wheezing, her legs shaking. Her muscles were weak, her reactions too slow, her skin mushroom white. For a predator, she was in very bad shape.

Dusk checked behind her. No Wolf. She wasn't being chased. Her heart stopped its wild hammering.

She checked in the other direction. And saw Prospect – a dead-end, dusty, one-street town, stuck with the research station in the middle of nowhere. No tourists ever came. The rest of the country didn't know it existed. Which was just how the military liked it. They needed local people to do the low paid jobs, like cleaning or garbage collection. But they liked to keep their affairs secret. They didn't want strangers sniffing around.

But to Dusk, imprisoned all her life in low laboratory buildings, Prospect seemed like paradise.

Her eyes zoomed in on the church, the tallest building she'd ever seen. Its steeple was a perfect lookout point. Up there she would feel safe. She could scan the ground, watch for danger, see everything that moved.

As she watched, a sparrowhawk went streaking in. It had prey in its talons. Dusk could identify it with her long-range vision. It was a mouse, like the one she'd just caught.

The sparrowhawk landed on the steeple. That was where Dusk wanted to be, high up, with the hawk.

'Home,' said Dusk, starting to walk towards Prospect.

Then she saw a dust cloud in the distance, heard the growl of jeep engines. It was the military.

She stopped walking. Waited obediently for them to find her, take her back to SERU. Then her head swivelled. *There!*

When the army convoy raced by, Dusk was out of sight in a drainage ditch, trying to catch a frog.

The frog flopped away. Dusk climbed out. Her fragile independence crumbled. She stared after the convoy. They'd left her behind. Who was going to look after her now? She almost threw herself on the ground and howled, she felt so lost, abandoned and afraid.

Dusk tugged at her hair. The hair slide had got tangled. It wouldn't come free. She screeched with rage and despair, began to claw at her arms.

Then her quick eyes saw something The grass glittered with gold. Smears, splashes, dribbles. The lab rats had been this way, scent-marking as they ran, rubbing their greasy coats on twigs and rocks. With her ultraviolet vision, Dusk could track their every move. Her hawk instincts kicked in.

'Dinner!' she said.

With her orange eyes bright and alert to everything around her, Dusk followed the General's army, and Wolf, into Prospect.

3

The City. Two Years Later . . .

Jay was sitting with his friends on the low car-park wall outside the supermarket. The security guard had just thrown them out, again.

Jay had complained, 'We only want to buy some Coke. Look, we got the money.' Jay had dug in his pocket, spread the coins across his hand to show him.

But the guard had said, 'On your way. You boys are trouble.'

Jay said, 'We weren't doing nothing!' And the guard had said, 'Yeah? Well, you ain't gonna get the chance. Not on my shift.'

He was watching them now, from just inside the entrance lobby, where the trolleys were stacked. So they were sitting on the wall, watching him back. After a while he got bored and went back to patrol the drinks section. Then there was nothing for Jay and his friends to do.

Jay yawned and said, 'I might be going to stay with my dad this summer.'

Someone said, 'He lives up in the wilderness, don't he? What you gonna do up there?'

Jay shrugged, 'Don't know for *definite* that I'm going up there yet. I haven't decided.'

Someone else sniggered, 'He's gonna go in the *woods*.' Woods were good for drinking beer and smoking dope and taking your girlfriend to have sex.

Jay said, 'Ma wants to get me away from you criminals.'

They laughed. But Jay knew it was true. Ma didn't like his friends. She thought they were bad boys. She was always talking about 'that gang you hang round with.' Trouble was, she didn't want him going to see Dad either. Dad was a bad influence too.

Jay had tried explaining about his friends. 'Ma, you don't know what you're talking about. We're not a gang. We're not even tough.'

In this city, gangs were known by the biggest psycho in the group. They had guns, knives, hatreds, territories. They ran drugs. Those gangs had girls who hung around practically begging you.

Jay thought, *I wish. If I had a Ma who chilled out more, I could tell her, 'Ma, all we do is smoke a little dope, do stupid things.'* Like spray paint a few walls, set off some car alarms.

But Ma thought even stuff like that would get you sent straight to Hell. So he ended up telling her wild, crazy things like, 'Hey Ma, we robbed some old ladies in wheel-chairs tonight!'

But he had to stop doing that because she'd clutch

a hand to her heart and say, 'Oh Jay! Please say you're kidding me!'

That hurt Jay a lot. That she actually thought that, maybe, he was capable of doing things like that.

Jay cuffed one of his friends round the head. Got cuffed back. He cuffed him again, got cuffed back. That got boring. He opened his mouth, yawned again, so his jaw almost dislocated. He was broke, fed up, restless. Couldn't even afford a pack of cigarettes and he only had one left. He needed something to happen.

The boy next to him nudged him in the ribs, 'Hey, look who's coming.'

It was Little Shane. He was called that to distinguish him from Big Shane, another guy in their school. And he was a loner, with no friends. No one knew much about him, except that he was addicted to comic books. He always carried one around, rolled up in his pocket. Sat on his own, reading it, mouthing the words.

Jay shouted out to Little Shane, 'Hey, you ponce.'

He didn't even know why he did it. Because he was bored. Because he wanted to show off, prove he was bad, like Ma thought he was.

Anyhow, at first it wasn't serious; it was just a joke. Just beating his chest, gorilla-style. He wasn't even taking a risk. He thought, *I could take him, easy.* Although, at that moment, he didn't intend to fight. It wouldn't be fair. Little Shane was a shrimp, a skinny little loser. No one had ever seen him even get mad. Let alone throw a punch.

'He's *weird*,' said one of Jay's friends. What went on inside Little Shane's head was a mystery. He hardly ever spoke. And when he did, it took him forever to get out the words. He never did anything in a hurry. He did everything in slow motion, like he had to think hard about it.

'Yeah, the guy shouldn't be allowed to live!' said Jay. But it was just his big mouth talking. He had nothing against Little Shane. He was weird but harmless. Jay had hardly noticed he existed, until now.

'You heard what I said?' Jay called out. 'You're a skinny little ponce. You're so skinny I could pick my teeth with you!'

Jay's friends laughed. That made Jay feel good.

But Little Shane didn't even turn his head. He just kept on trudging by, slow as a tortoise, minding his own business, like Jay didn't exist.

Jay got resentful then, that he was being ignored. He thought, *Hasn't the guy got any feelings? Where's his self respect? He'll just take anything.*

'You're a skinny little ponce!' shouted Jay, his insults getting wilder, his mouth out of control. 'And you have sex with your mother. You know what that makes you!'

Jay turned round, grinning, excited, for his friends' approval. 'You heard what I just said?'

Then one of his friends said, 'Watch out.' This time Little Shane did react. He'd turned his head. And his face had transformed, from a thirteen-year-old kid's face into a monster's. It was screwed up, mean and menacing. His eyes blazed with pure savagery.

Jay had never seen rage like it. It was primitive. He wasn't prepared. He was taken completely by surprise.

He swallowed, hard. His stomach felt like it was

31

hurtling down a deep, dark pit. He almost threw up, right there in the car park. He knew, instantly, he'd picked on the wrong kid. Made a major error of judgement.

Little Shane did have feelings, after all.

'What did I say? What did I say?' he hissed, out the corner of his mouth.

One of his friends shrugged. 'Don't ask me.'

Another said, 'He don't even have a mum. She ran off with someone.'

Then there was no time for talk. Little Shane could move fast, when he chose to. He was charging at Jay, his head down, like a little bull.

Jay was beat from the start. He was caught completely off guard. And there was no way he could summon up Little Shane's level of hatred. It just wasn't in him.

Little Shane sprang on Jay's back, scratching, biting, spitting. Kicking Jay in the kidneys with his boots. He seemed to have superhuman strength, like one of his comic-book characters.

And Jay couldn't even begin to defend himself. He was overwhelmed. Little Shane's attack was so ferocious, so violent.

He staggered about, trying to shake off Little Shane. But he was blinded. Little Shane had wrapped his arms round Jay's head, like octopus tentacles. It must have looked comical. Jay could hear his friends laughing. Even cheering Little Shane on: 'Look at that little guy. He's crazy!'

Little Shane wouldn't budge. He was clinging on with his left arm, smashing his right fist into Jay's face, again and again. Blood pumped from Jay's nose. His face and

Little Shane's fist were slippery with it. But Little Shane carried on punching. His hard, bony knuckles were like pistons.

'Get him off me!' Jay shouted, wildly, throwing windmill punches that didn't connect. He tried to rip Little Shane's arms from round his throat. But Little Shane clung on, squeezing tighter. Jay couldn't breathe. There was a red mist in front of his eyes. Salty blood filled his mouth, choked him.

He sank to his knees, with Little Shane still throttling him.

Jay thought, *I'm dying*.

Then Jay's friends stepped in. One said to little Shane, 'He's had enough.'

And quick as it had started, it stopped. Little Shane seemed to lose interest. He loosed his grip on Jay's throat and scuttled away on all fours, like a crab. He didn't even run off. He sat on the car-park wall, just metres away, took a comic book out his pocket, began reading it. As if the whole thing had never happened.

Jay was still on his knees, swaying, his head in his hands, blood trickling from between his fingers.

'You all right?' said one of his friends, shaking him. 'Jay? Did he bust your nose?'

Another said, 'Can you believe that? See what that guy Shane just did?' He sounded horrified but impressed.

'I'm all right. I'm all right,' said Jay, pushing them away. 'Just leave me alone.'

'Shall I call your Ma?' said someone. 'Tell her to come get you?'

'Just leave me alone!' screamed Jay.

He didn't know how he made it back home. His brain wasn't working. It was numb with pain and shock. But his legs kept walking. Like they didn't belong to him. He went down alleyways, kept out of sight. Even so, he felt the whole world was staring at him.

Halfway, he stopped, leaned against a wheelie bin. He was sick, heaving his guts up, until there was nothing left in his stomach and he was just bringing up sour bile. At last what had happened seem to strike home. 'I got beat up, by Little Shane.' He hadn't landed one punch. His hands weren't even bruised. But now he smashed his fists into a wall, again and again, until his knuckles were scraped raw and bleeding.

He leaned against the wall, weak and shivering. He thought of calling his dad on his mobile. Dismissed the idea straightaway. Curtis was five hundred miles away. What could he do? And anyway, he was probably drunk. So Jay lit his last cigarette instead. His hands were shaking so much it took him three tries. He took a deep drag, ground it out under his heel. Then staggered on home.

He wanted to sneak into the flat, clean himself up. But no chance. Ma was on him as soon as he opened the door. 'Look at your face! What happened to you?'

Jay stumbled past her. 'Don't start, Ma! I'm all right.' He shut himself in his bedroom. Then, all at once, he was shivering and crying, smearing his face with blood and tears.

It was a while before he could pull himself together, before he dared look in his bedroom mirror.

He could see why Ma had gone berserk. His face was a mess. He touched his cheek tenderly. It was swollen, lumpy. His T-shirt was soaked with blood – it was his favourite one too. He felt his nose. 'Shit!' It hurt like hell. He just hoped it wasn't busted.

He went out of his bedroom to face Ma. He had to do it some time. She'd probably been listening at his bedroom door, pacing outside all this time. He wanted Ma to be cool, play it down, not start getting hysterical. He felt if she did that, he might burst into tears all over again. But Ma was predictable.

'You've been in a fight! Just look at your hands!'

Jay took a deep shaky breath, struggled to hold himself together. 'You ought to see the other guy!' he boasted. 'After I got finished with him.'

Ma started preaching. 'The Bible says –'

Jay lost it again. 'I don't care what the bloody Bible says!' he shrieked at her, demented.

'I'm going to call the police! The boy who did this to you should be punished!'

'Just mind your own business, Ma. You don't know what you're talking about!'

He couldn't say, 'I asked for it. I practically made him do it.'

Jay slammed back into his bedroom. Paced around it like a trapped, wounded animal. Switched on his TV. The noise hurt his head. He couldn't stand it. He switched it off, picked up a magazine. The edge of a page sliced his finger. Only a little cut, but deep and it stung like crazy. But it was the last straw. It broke him completely.

And suddenly he was crying again, great, gulping, body-shaking sobs. All the awful consequences of what had just happened, the humiliation, hit him like an express train.

'He destroyed you!' he sobbed, rocking backwards and forwards. 'He totally destroyed you. In front of all your friends! And you just stood there, let him do it!'

Jay knew his friends would be phoning other kids now, telling them about it. It was too good a story not to share. He could just imagine it. *Yeah, honest, I'm telling you the truth! Jay really got his ass kicked! By Little Shane! Yeah, I couldn't believe it either! And I was there!*

That night, instead of sleeping, he kept reliving the fight in his head. Over and over and over. It made him squirm and sweat every time. But he couldn't shut his mind down. It seemed like the night was never going to end. At last the light in his bedroom grew pale and fuzzy. It was dawn. He was so weary he could have screamed, so sick to death of seeing the fight in every cringe-making detail. But here it came again, one more time, to torment him. He still couldn't believe it – Little Shane's explosion of pure savagery. Still couldn't believe he'd been so unprepared. And it was all his own fault. He'd asked for it. Set himself up. If he hadn't made Little Shane mad, said that about his mother . . .

Shut up! he told his brain. He dragged himself out of bed, padded to the bathroom to have a shower. His own face stared back at him from the mirror. 'What a mess,' he groaned.

He'd thought the bruises would fade overnight, like

36

they did on TV. But they were worse today. The one on his cheekbone was deep purple. His nose was puffed up, like a clown's.

How was he going to face them all at school today? He'd been one of the cool guys before. Not the most popular or anything, but still respected. He'd been happy with that, felt easy in his own skin. But now his reputation was nil, his credibility zero. There were certain kids who would never let him live this down. He could already hear their cruel, mocking voices in his head.

Hey, Jay, I heard Little Shane beat you up, Better pick on my baby sister next time.

He came out of the bathroom dressed. He was going to skip breakfast – he wasn't hungry anyhow – and slip past Ma. But she was up. Already cleaning before she went to her job, cleaning rich people's houses. She pretended to be shining the kitchen taps but, soon as she heard his footsteps, she was on him.

'You're not going to school today, are you?'

'Yes,' said Jay. He'd thought about it, taking the day off, the week off. Never going back. But he couldn't let himself do that. His respect for himself was already at rock bottom. *Do you want to be even more of a loser?* he'd taunted himself. But there was another reason too. Whatever happened at school today, he deserved all he got. He just had to take his punishment, get it over with.

Ma turned round, with her yellow rubber gloves on. She had that preachy look on her face. She opened her mouth. Jay said, 'Don't tell me nothing about Jesus! I'm not in the mood for all that religious crap!'

Ever since Ma and Curtis had split up, six years ago, Ma had spent even more time at chapel.

Jay said, 'I'm warning you, Ma!' He couldn't control himself just now, couldn't be kind. In fact he needed to hurt someone, really badly. And he knew, just knew, it was going to be Ma.

'I told you, I don't believe in God or Jesus. I don't believe in nothing.'

Ma peeled off her gloves. 'Jesus loves you anyway,' she told him, with that long-suffering, patient smile that made him want to hurt her even more. 'You should tell Him your problems.'

'But I don't believe in him! I just told you!'

'He still loves you. He's watching you all the time.'

'What is he? Some kind of creepy pervert?' asked Jay.

'He's got a plan for your life,' Ma insisted. 'Just trust Him.'

Jay thought, *Why won't she shut up?* But Ma couldn't shut up about Jesus. He was like her best friend.

'This fight you were in —' she started saying.

'It wasn't a fight!' Jay screamed at her. 'And I got my own plan for my own life. Just tell your Jesus to butt out! Mind his own damn business!'

Ma went silent. She looked hurt, bewildered. They didn't understand each other. There were oceans between them — her beliefs put oceans between them. But Jay still loved her. At least she hadn't left him, like Curtis had.

Usually Jay felt guilty when he upset Ma. She was such an easy target. This morning, though, there were demons inside him, driving him on. He felt vicious, murderous, like he wanted to rip someone's head off.

'Why should I trust him anyway? He's a total loser! Look what a mess he's made of the world. People hurting each other. Shitty things happening . . .'

Ma's lips pressed into a stubborn line. 'He still loves you,' she said. 'Nothing you say can change that.'

'*I – don't – believe – in – him!* Why don't you ever *listen*?'

Jay felt like screaming. *Aaaaargh!* Arguing with Ma about religion just made him feel worse. It always drove him wild with frustration. Why hadn't he remembered that? He could never win. They just went round in circles.

'I'm definitely, I mean *definitely*, going to see Dad this summer,' Jay told Ma as he crashed the door shut behind him.

By the Chinese food store opposite, some of his friends were hanging around, waiting to see if he would show up. When they saw him, he could see their eyes light up.

Someone sniggered, 'He looks like he's been hit by a truck!'

'It don't look that bad, Jay,' someone else tried to reassure him. The pity in his voice was worse than the sniggering.

Jay shut his eyes, swallowed hard. It felt like there was a stone in his throat he couldn't shift. He wanted a cloak of invisibility. Wanted to crawl under a rock and die. Instead, he opened his eyes again. Said, 'Hey guys.' And crossed the road to meet them.

4

Jay sat on a pile of logs at the turn-off, waiting for Curtis to pick him up.

He was wearing his favourite baggy white T-shirt. Ma had got out the blood with a Stain Devil. It was far too big for him. Extra Large. But that's how he liked it. He had army shorts on and trainers with no socks. His black baseball cap had a Japanese character on it, embroidered in silver. The guy on the market stall had told him it meant 'Number One'. Jay had the cap pulled down low on his head. He had a plaited leather cord round his neck, with three grey metal dice threaded on it. A backpack, his only luggage, was down by his feet.

It was two weeks since he'd been beat up by Little Shane. The bruises had gone from purple and blue to green, then yellow. Then faded altogether. His face was back to normal. His T-shirt was washed sparkling white. But inside, Jay hadn't recovered.

He told himself, *It's no big deal. Some kids get beat up every day.* But he just couldn't get over it. He was a changed person.

Jay had been travelling all day, on three different buses.

He felt gritty and hot and tired. The last one, a wheezing old country bus, had dropped him here forty minutes ago and rattled off, in a cloud of dust. Jay was smoking his last cigarette.

There was a general store across the road. Just a shack, standing all on its own. But it was closed and shuttered. At six o'clock in the evening!

Shitty dump, thought Jay. He should have bought more supplies. It hadn't occurred to him that cigarettes would be hard to get. Back in the city, shops were open 24/7. You could buy anything you wanted, any time of the day or night.

Jay stubbed out the cigarette. He was getting fidgety now. He kicked his heels against the logs. Swatted the gnats trying to drown themselves in his eyes.

He checked his watch. Dad had said he'd be here. He tried phoning for the third time. Couldn't even raise Dad's mobile. *He's probably forgotten I'm coming. Probably drunk out of his skull*, thought Jay.

Drink was the main reason Curtis and Ma had split up. It was Curtis who went roaming off, never came back. He'd got worse in the last two years. Since SERU, the place where he worked, burned down. After that he was even more of a loser. His whole life just fell apart.

'Not again,' groaned Jay. That dreary reel in his head, the one that ran and reran the fight with Little Shane, had started. Jay was sick to death of it. But he had no control over it. He could already feel himself squirming.

To try and make it stop, he scrabbled in his backpack, took a box of matches out of the front pocket.

41

He started playing the pain game. He'd seen other kids playing it before. He'd always thought it was for morons or masochists. Now he was playing it himself. He'd started in his bedroom, when he'd come home from that first day at school after the fight with Little Shane.

It had been the worst day of his life. Everybody knew all the sordid details. They must have been texting each other all night. He could practically hear the girls giggling behind his back. The best-looking one said, 'See his face? Little Shane did that. Yeah, Little Shane was riding around on his back! Beat him up good. Can you believe it? I mean, the shame!'

Jay heard it all. He was meant to hear it. And he'd been going to ask her for a date. He'd thought, before the fight, that his chances were pretty good.

He was sure Little Shane would cash in on his victory. Go swaggering round, crowing, 'You shoulda seen me. He was pathetic. I kicked his ass!' But he didn't. Kids gave Little Shane much more respect. But he acted like he didn't even need it. He was just his usual weird slow-motion self, sitting apart, minding his own business, reading his comic books. That made it even harder to bear. Like he didn't think beating up Jay was any big deal. When, for Jay, it was the biggest deal, ever.

Jay put three matches between the fingers of his left hand. With his right hand he struck another match on a log. He lit the three matches. The skin between the fingers of both hands was already scabbed with burns that were trying to heal. He held his left hand out. The trick was to keep it rock steady while you tested yourself, to see how long you could stand it.

As the matches burned down, his hand began to shake slightly. He was breathing harder, anticipating pain.

Here it came! His face screwed up but he forced himself to keep his hand level. For about two seconds.

Then he couldn't stand it. He shook the matches out, nursed his burnt hand, rocking backwards and forwards.

'Shit, shit, shit, shit.'

That didn't hurt enough. It wasn't enough pain. Next time, he'd let those matches burn down, all the way.

He tried calling Dad again. No contact. He squinted up the dirt road. No sign of him.

Why did Dad move up here? wondered Jay. It felt like he'd been dumped at the end of the world.

I'll give him ten minutes more, he thought. *Then I'll start walking.*

It was five miles to Dad's cabin. There were already pink streaks in the sky. The sun would be setting soon.

The minutes passed. It was so silent here, it was spooky. No traffic noise, no car horns, no sound at all. Just bees humming in some purple flowers, next to him.

Still Curtis didn't show up.

Jay thought, *Wonder if he's still driving that old four-by-four?* He hoped so. Jay had taught himself to drive in that thing. Curtis had let him on his last visit. Ma would have a fit if she knew. But up here there were plenty of kids, younger than he was, driving beat-up trucks around these back roads. If the police knew, they turned a blind eye.

There was a harsh, wild cry from the woods. Jay

jumped up, startled. What was it, some kind of bird?

Better start walking, he told himself. He could feel the hairs prickling at the back of his neck. He looked over his shoulder, as if he suspected someone was watching him. There was nothing but forest. Not a living soul anywhere.

He felt better when he was striding out.

He called Ma to moan, 'Dad didn't pick me up.' He just wanted to hear a human voice. But Ma's mobile was off. Maybe she was still at work. Those rich ladies wouldn't let her take personal calls.

He thought about phoning one of his friends. But they hadn't been phoning or texting him lately. Hadn't been coming round to his house. It was like, after Little Shane, he had leprosy or something. One second he told himself he was imagining it – that they didn't want to know him. Then the next second he felt like an outcast.

He told himself, *It'll be all right after the summer. They'll have forgotten about it.* One second he was confident about that. The next he wasn't.

What he *did* want was to turn back time. So everything was like it was before he'd opened his big mouth.

He tried Ma one more time. He tried Curtis. No answer from anyone. He gave up, put his mobile away.

Jay stopped trudging. Looked around. He'd been so busy with his phone, trying to reach someone, that he hadn't been paying attention. He wasn't on the wide dirt track he'd started out on. He'd somehow wandered off it, on to a grassy side path that led between the trees.

I'm lost, thought Jay.

He felt that chill again, at the back of his neck. Those

pine trees crowded around him, dense and sombre and dark green. They seemed to be moving closer, whispering together. It was like being trapped at the bottom of a deep, narrow canyon. He couldn't even see the sky.

These woods stretched for miles. If people got lost here, Curtis had told him, sometimes their bodies stayed missing for years. They'd found a plane somewhere in the woods – with the skeleton of a pilot inside – that had crashed in 1943.

And Jay had worse fears than that. He'd seen films where kids from the city stumbled into the woods. Usually their car ran out of fuel. And there was some kind of mutant redneck clan with chainsaws and scythes who hunted them down, one by one.

Don't get panicky, Jay told himself. *I've got my mobile. I can call for help.* He got his phone out of his backpack again.

But he didn't need it. His next step took him out of the trees on to a dirt track again. There was a house. Jay sighed with relief.

What if he'd called out the emergency services, helicopters, search parties, the whole lot? 'Come and rescue me! I'm scared of guys with chainsaws!' When he was so close to civilization!

I'd have looked like the biggest wuss in the world, decided Jay, putting his mobile away. He didn't want to look like that twice in his life.

The house was reassuring. The kind you weren't scared to ask directions at.

Not like Dad's place, thought Jay.

Dad's place was a real dump. It looked like a scrap-yard with junk and rusty cars everywhere. If you were a stranger, lost in the woods, there's no way you'd knock on Curtis's front door.

But this place looked welcoming, like a gingerbread cottage. A neat little house with shutters and roses round the door. And even a dove house in the front garden.

He saw a lady watering her roses. Not young, maybe as old as Ma. A nice lady, friendly-looking, with faded brown hair piled into a bun.

Encouraged, Jay walked up to the gate. There was nothing to be scared of here.

Then he stopped. Outside the yard, facing the road, was a wooden cross. And pinned to it, with its wings pathetically outstretched, was a dead hawk.

It gave Jay a big shock. He felt confused and slightly sick. The crucified bird didn't fit in with the nice, smiling lady and the picture-postcard cottage. He stared at the hawk. Its head drooped on to its chest. Its open eyes had lost all their brightness – they had a dull bluish tinge. Flies and tiny spiders crawled through its feathers.

Jay gulped down the bile rising in his throat. The lady came bustling over, wiping her hands. Smiling sweetly at him, 'Hello, son.' She seemed very friendly. But Jay couldn't take his eyes off that hawk.

'Yep, I got another one,' said the lady, seeing him staring at it.

Jay thought, *I don't want to know about this*. He just wanted to ask directions and get out of here. But the lady told him anyway.

'They're dead when I nail 'em up,' she said brightly.

Jay thought, *That's not so bad.* It was probably some weird country custom.

Then she told him, 'I poison 'em. All you have to do is, you take a wild pigeon. Put some poison on its feathers. Stake it out. Better if you break one of its wings first. Then the hawk sees it struggling to fly. Comes down to kill it. And then *he's* dead! Works every time!'

She nodded her head proudly. 'I hate those hawks. I'd like to wipe out every single one of them. Think they can kill my doves and get away with it . . .'

Jay's eyes moved mechanically to the dove house. Outside it, on a ledge, three pretty white doves were fluttering and cooing.

Jay had to ask her; he just couldn't stop himself, 'Why do you hang 'em up like that?'

She looked at him as if he was some kind of idiot. 'Why, as a warning to other hawks, of course.'

Jay thought, *What is she? A ghoul?* Disguised as a nice country lady. With a sweet, welcoming smile.

He wanted to argue with her, like he did with Ma. Make her see sense. 'What's the use of doing that? Hawks don't think like we do. How do they know it's a warning?'

But she scared him – that kindly smile and that blood-thirsty gleam in her eyes.

'Sometimes,' she told him, 'I got three of them hanging up there, all in a row!'

Jay backed off. Broke into a stumbling run.

'Did you want something, son?' she called after him.

But Jay just wanted to escape. When he was in the

47

woods and the cottage was behind him, he stopped. *I was supposed to ask the way.* But he couldn't bring himself to go back there. See that dead bird, crucified by a sweet, smiling lady.

Jay just knew, with a kind of weary resignation, that the dead hawk was going to be one of those images that his mind showed him again and again. Even though he didn't want it to. Just like what happened with Little Shane.

Jay suddenly realized there were no trees around him. The woods had let him go.

But in front of him, just a few metres away, was a high wire fence. It was covered with signs. WARNING! they shrieked at him in huge, red letters. BIO HAZARD! DANGER. ELECTRIFIED FENCE. DO NOT ENTER!

5

Jay was careful not to get too close. He looked through the high-wire fence. What he saw was buildings smothered by creepers, crushed under their weight. Tree roots bursting through the tarmac of the main street. He saw a church steeple, still standing, wound round and round with creepers.

Jay thought, *I know where this is*. This was Prospect. It had once been a town. Now it was a green wilderness. He'd never been here. But Curtis had told him what happened .

It was on Jay's last visit. For some reason, Curtis had taken him to the research station where he used to work until two years ago, when the whole place went sky high.

Jay had said, 'What are we here for, Dad?'

But Curtis hadn't answered. He'd gazed around with haunted eyes. Kicked at a few bits of scorched and blackened concrete.

There was nothing to see. They'd razed all the buildings to the ground after the fire. There was nothing to identify what it had been. Except for a forgotten sign Jay picked up, lying in the grass. It was corroded, bleached by the sun, but you could still make out the letters: SERU.

'What's that mean?' asked Jay, not much interested.

'Sensory Enhancement Research Unit,' Curtis had told him.

'So what did you do there, Dad?' Jay had always been hazy about that. He knew it was some army base, that's all.

Curtis had tapped his nose. 'Top Secret, son. National Security. I ain't allowed to talk about it.'

Jay had said, sarcastically, 'No kidding.' He thought Dad was lying. Trying to make himself look big and important, like he was some kind of undercover agent or international spy.

It was then Curtis had told him about Prospect. He'd said, 'There used to be a town here, just down the road.'

After SERU exploded, the army men had evacuated Prospect. Gone racing there in jeeps and made all the people leave.

'What did they do that for?' Jay had asked Curtis.

'They said the drinking water was toxic,' Curtis told him. 'They said the radioactive isotopes they used for research at SERU had polluted the town's water supply. The military'll tell you any old bullshit.'

'What, you mean it wasn't true?'

But Curtis wasn't saying any more, except, 'They had their reasons. It was Top Secret.'

Jay had lost interest. 'Yeah, yeah, Dad,' he'd said, sighing. 'Top Secret.'

He'd even wondered if Prospect really existed or if Dad had been making it all up. But here he was, looking through the wire. And it was all just like Dad said – the abandoned town, the warning signs.

Dad said the signs were lies, Jay reminded himself. *That there was no radioactivity.*

Not that he intended to test that out. You couldn't take Curtis's word for anything. He was always saying things he didn't mean. Promising things he didn't deliver. Like, 'I'll come and spend Christmas with you and Ma.' Or, 'I'll send you a big fat cheque on your birthday.' And when you were little you never learned. Every time, you believed him. Thought he was going to keep his promises. And every time, he let you down.

In any case, Jay thought, *even if I were fool enough to want to go into Prospect, there's still the electrified fence stopping me.* Jay shrugged and turned away. The main thing was, he'd got his bearings. SERU, or where it once was, was about a mile down the road. When he got there it was twenty minutes' walk to Dad's place. He'd be at the cabin before nightfall.

And darkness wasn't that far away. It was already twilight. It looked different here than in the city. In the city you didn't even notice it. But here the whole landscape was dissolving into ghostly greyness. Shapes blurred into each other. It was eerie, unsettling. You couldn't tell what was real and what wasn't. Was that something moving between the trees, or just shadows?

Jay began walking along quickly, following the fence.

Dusk was crouching in the window of the church steeple she'd made her home. There'd been stained glass in it once.

But that had long ago shattered and fallen out. Now creepers almost choked the window. Dusk had to clear them every now and again, so she had somewhere to perch.

On an ivy-covered ledge outside, a sparrowhawk sat on her nest. She didn't seem disturbed by Dusk. Dusk mewed at her affectionately. The hawk mewed back. Then sat with her eyes closed and let the wind ruffle her feathers.

There was a sudden screech. The sparrowhawk's mate landed on the nest and passed a gift of food from his hooked beak into hers. It was a wriggling lizard. The female wouldn't leave her eggs. If he didn't feed her she would starve.

When Dusk saw him streaking in like an arrow, that same old longing tugged at her heart.

She squatted on the window ledge like a stone gargoyle, her long shaggy hair bleached white by the sun, her orange eyes fierce with yearning.

Maybe, this time, she would just tip herself, spread out her arms and fly. Sometimes she had absolute faith . . .

Then her hawk eyes zoomed from wide angle to close up. She'd seen something.

'Boy!' she said. She swivelled her head, uneasily.

There were no people in Prospect. The army men drove them all out. Dusk had watched it from her tower.

They'd thrown a fence round the entire town. It hadn't taken them long. Prospect was a modest place: one shop, one bank, one filling station, one church, a few houses. Population 593 at the last count. Now the population was one person. If you decided to count Dusk as human.

Dusk kept well away from that fence. It fried you to a

52

black crisp if you tried to climb it. She'd seen it happen to a rat.

After the town was empty, some soldiers had come in. They'd carried guns. They went in all the buildings. They seemed to be searching for something. But when they climbed the steeple, Dusk had hidden up in the rafters, flattened against a beam. She watched the search party as they stamped about, raising the dust.

'Nothing here,' said one. Then they left.

They'd shot a dog dead before they went. It rushed out at them snarling. Frothing at the mouth. It wasn't Wolf they killed – Dusk was pleased about that.

The search parties had come a couple more times. Dusk always hid from them. Sometimes, like the boy she was watching, people came and gawped through the fence. Dusk hid from them too. She'd made her home here, with the hawks and other wild creatures. She didn't want anything to do with people.

Except sometimes she'd take out her hair slide. She'd clean it with spit, watch it sparkle. Among all the bad memories she'd got of SERU, Curtis's small act of kindness shone out in her mind as bright as those glass diamonds.

While the female sparrowhawk daintily teased out the lizard's guts, Dusk focused on the boy. The fence was 400 metres away, across open scrubland. The light was fading. To Jay, the church tower was fuzzy, indistinct. But Dusk could see the silver 'Number One' glitter on his cap. That's how she tracked his movements. And he was moving away.

Dusk relaxed. She hadn't really thought he was a threat. All the threats she faced were inside Prospect. She even grinned. Dusk called after him, knowing he was much too far away to hear. 'Run away!' she told him.

She didn't take prey his size. But there were other predators beside her in Prospect.

Then she forgot him. People weren't important. She didn't depend on them any more; she looked after herself.

Food! she was thinking.

She felt a rush of adrenalin. Food always gave her that buzz. She slid her third eyelids over her eyes and back again.

It was twilight, the time when Dusk could see best. When her main food source, mice and voles, came out. But it was only a brief slot of time. When twilight ended, when darkness came down, she had to hurry back to the tower. That's when the rats came out to hunt. She had to be back in the tower by nightfall. Night belonged to the rats.

6

'How did you get here?' asked Curtis. He looked at Jay out of bleary eyes.

Jay had just shaken him awake. Curtis had been asleep on his front porch. There was a whisky bottle down by his side.

'You were supposed to pick me up,' said Jay.

'Well, good heavens,' said Curtis, looking at his watch. 'Is that the time?'

Curtis started apologizing. But Jay didn't even feel that angry. He was so used to Curtis letting him down that he hardly reacted to it any more.

'When did you last eat?' said Jay, dumping his backpack.

Curtis looked vague. 'I can't remember.' He looked a wreck. His eyes watery and bloodshot.

Jay went into the house. 'And look at the state of this place,' he said. 'It's like a garbage tip in here.' Dirty clothes, dirty crockery all over the place. 'Don't you ever clean up, Dad?'

Jay tutted and shook his head. He fussed around like Ma, picking things up, wiping up beer spills on the floor.

He gave Curtis a hard time about it. 'Pigs wouldn't even live in this place.'

'And how much you been drinking?' Jay demanded.

He picked up the whisky bottle from the side of Curtis's bed and shook it. It was empty.

It was one way he could cope with Curtis, pretending that he was the parent and Curtis was a weak and helpless baby who needed looking after. Sometimes, he'd make excuses for Curtis. *He can't help it.* Sometimes, he'd get resentful and furious. He'd turn on Curtis: 'You're pathetic, Dad. Your life is a mess. You got to get a grip!' But it was like kicking a sick puppy – he always felt guilty afterwards, because Curtis just agreed with him. He'd nod, in a self-pitying sort of way. 'You're right, son. I'm going to cut down. Tomorrow, I promise.' Then he'd open another whisky bottle.

'How's your Ma?' asked Curtis, hauling himself out of the broken cane chair he'd been sitting in and shambling into the house. 'She still talking to Jesus?'

'Ma's fine,' said Jay.

Jay had hurt Ma a lot, especially after he'd taken the beating. He'd said mean, unforgivable things. But he didn't think Curtis had any right to say mean things about Ma.

Ma had stayed around when Curtis left. Ma was reliable, steady like a rock. She would never, ever leave you stranded, forget to pick you up. She'd turn up ten minutes early and be waiting, so you wouldn't get worried.

And anyway, once he had asked her that same question, just to wind her up: 'You still talking to Jesus, Ma?'

And she'd said, 'Who else is going to listen to me?'

Sometimes Jay wished, like Ma, he had someone he believed in, who was wise and powerful, to tell all his troubles to. When he was little and went to Sunday school and said his prayers he thought God was like that. But then he'd got older, smarter, less easy to fool. Now, just like he didn't believe in Curtis, he didn't believe in God either. Sometimes he thought, *Isn't there anybody, anywhere who doesn't mess up?*

Jay looked in the fridge. There was nothing in there but cans of beer. Wait a minute, behind them was an unopened box of hamburgers. How long had that been there? Jay didn't want to look at the sell-by date. He just got out the frying pan.

'Dad, how many burgers you want?'

Next morning, Jay tried to shake Curtis awake. Curtis groaned and turned over. Curtis had been good last night. He hadn't drunk in front of Jay – except for a beer or two. He hated Jay's disapproving stare. He thought, *It's just like Ma's.* He'd only started serious drinking after Jay went to bed.

Jay shook his head sadly. He'd known all along that's what Curtis planned to do. He wasn't even angry. He felt almost sorry for Curtis. Poor Dad. He just didn't realize his son had grown up, wasn't so easy to fool any more.

Jay tried again. 'Where's the nearest store? Is it the one back at the turn-off?'

He wanted breakfast. Back home he didn't even have to think about it. Ma made sure there was always stuff in the fridge, all his favourite things. But more urgently, he wanted cigarettes. He'd already searched the cabin.

Curtis kept all sort of rubbish: old unpaid bills from years back, half-used, melted candles. In one drawer, something red winked at him. It was a cheap hair slide, made out of pink plastic, sparkling with fake glass rubies.

Sighing, Jay threw it back in the drawer with all the other junk. No good asking Curtis why he'd kept that. He wouldn't even remember.

Jay shook Dad again, more violently this time. 'And where's the car keys?' asked Jay. He'd looked for them when he'd been searching for cigarettes, hadn't found them.

He couldn't wait to drive the four-by-four round those forest tracks. See if he remembered how to.

Curtis trembled like a dog in his sleep. He must have been dreaming. He was saying something.

'What?' said Jay, putting his ear close to Curtis's face.

But it wasn't the name of the nearest cigarette shop or where he'd put the car keys.

'Poor little freak,' moaned Curtis. 'Why'd they do that to her?'

'What little freak?' said Jay, shaking Curtis's limp arm.

'I shoulda kept hold of her. She never had a chance . . .'

Then his words slurred, became mumbling. You couldn't make them out. Jay let Curtis's arm drop. He tucked it inside the blanket. It flopped out again. Jay tucked it back in, gently, so Curtis didn't get cold.

The cabin was stuffy. It smelled of sweaty bodies and stale, greasy food. Jay wanted to escape. He scribbled on a piece of paper: *Gone to turn-off to get food.* He stuck it on the fridge door where Curtis was sure to find it when he went to get his first cold beer of the day. Then he stepped out into the clear, fresh morning.

He took great lungfuls of country air. There was dew sparkling on the grass in Curtis's front yard. In the east, the sky showed slashes of pink like a sliced-open watermelon.

It's just after dawn! thought Jay, amazed. Why had he got up so early? He hadn't got up as early as this in his entire life.

He was about to go back to bed when something whined, down at his feet.

'Hey, boy!' said Jay. It was a mangy dog, its ribs showing, crawling on its belly round his legs.

Jay thought, *It looks like a stray.* Then he wondered, *Does it belong to Dad?* Surely Curtis would have fed it sometimes, not let it get into this state? But Jay wasn't sure about that. He sighed. Another thing he had to take responsibility for. 'I'll get it some dog food, at the store,' he decided.

Jay went back into the house. *There's no way I'm using my own money*, he thought. Searching through Curtis's jeans – in a crumpled heap on the floor – he found some cash but no car keys.

Jay sighed, 'I'm going to have to walk.'

The dog was waiting for him outside.

'Stay here,' said Jay to the dog. He knelt down. It was some kind of hound. People used them for hunting round here. Its eyes were big and brown and liquid, like Bambi's.

It licked his hand, sniffed around him, learning his scent.

'*Awwww*, shit,' said Jay. 'Suppose you want to come with me?' The dog thumped its tail feebly. 'We've got to walk,' Jay warned it.

He was already feeling twitchy for that first cigarette of the day.

Jay didn't feel comfortable with animals. He didn't even like them much. He'd never owned one. Pets weren't allowed in their apartment.

He put on his cap, pulled it low down on his head. Checked he had some matches in his pocket. All his friends used disposable lighters but you couldn't do the pain game with lighters. Not the way he liked to play it anyway.

'Come on, dog,' said Jay.

Gloomy pines crowded in on them. Daylight hadn't reached here yet. There were still deep pools of black shadow between the trees. Jay wasn't sorry to have the dog trotting beside him.

'You hungry?' he asked it. 'I'll get you something to eat.' He wondered what its name was.

Curtis shouldn't be allowed to have a dog, he thought. *He can't even get food in for his own kid.*

The woods looked more welcoming now. Shafts of sunlight poured down. The dark, cold pools between trees changed to warm gold.

There was a sudden break in the pines, a wide grassy avenue. Jay looked down it. There was the gingerbread cottage. And the lady with the sweet, friendly smile, out watering her roses before the heat of the day shrivelled them.

She waved and shouted. 'Hi there, son. You're out bright and early this morning.'

Jay waved back. *You cruel bitch*, he was thinking, as he gave her a big smile. She poisoned hawks; she broke the wings of pigeons.

He was too far away to see the sad bundle of feathers hanging from her home-made cross. But he could see it in his mind. As he pictured it, those tiny spiders he'd seen crawling in its feathers had spun sparkling, silvery webs all over it. Made it something beautiful. As if it had conquered cruelty and death . . .

Jay shuddered to shake away the image. He didn't like it when his mind got mystical. It unsettled him. *Just concentrate on the road. Right?* he ordered himself. He didn't want to get lost in the woods again.

The dog was trotting right beside him, as if it had belonged to him all its life. It was scabby and skinny. The kind of dog you'd see in the city sniffing around garbage sacks.

It could be a good dog though, thought Jay. *If somebody took care of it.*

The dog didn't have a collar. Jay untied the plaited leather cord from round his neck. Tied it round the dog's neck instead.

'That's a cool collar,' Jay told it.

It was like he'd claimed the dog for his own, adopted it.

Suddenly the dog stiffened. Its nose quivered. It had seen something through the trees. Yelping madly, it dashed off.

'Hey!' yelled Jay. He started running after it, crashing through branches. He couldn't lose it. It was his dog now.

He ran on squashy layers of pine needles, through dappled sunlight, following the sound of barking. 'Here, boy!'

Then he didn't hear the barking any more. Jay came bursting out of the trees. He saw a skull and crossbones. DANGER! the sign shrieked at him. RADIOACTIVE WATER!

He was back at Prospect again but not at the same place. This time, when he looked through the fence he saw a big pond glinting through trees. White waterlilies gleamed on its surface like stars.

But Dad says it isn't radioactive, Jay reminded himself. *He says the military was lying.*

He couldn't see any reason why they should do that. But it was hard to believe a pond so serene and lovely could be poisoned. Looking through the wire, the whole of Prospect seemed like a peaceful green paradise.

Jay looked for the dog, saw him much further along the fence. He seemed to be digging something up.

Jay started running. *Hope he stays away from that fence*, he was thinking. *He'll get fried.*

Behind Jay, there was a sinister ripple on the pond. A ripple made by something big. A scaly snout with two nostrils lifted the waterlily leaves. Then sank back again into the depths.

When Jay reached him, the dog was barking, scrabbling at the soil. 'What's up?' said Jay. 'What you found?'

The dog was trying to dig up a big rock, like he was desperate to know what was underneath it. Using all his strength, Jay heaved it aside for him. 'That what you want?'

The dog started digging again, his front paws a blur,

soil flying all around him. Jay saw the end of a red pipe, some kind of storm drain. It was still blocked though. He pulled some small rocks out, saw an opening. It seemed to lead into Prospect under the electric fence.

'You don't want to go in there,' Jay told his dog. 'You'll get cancer.'

But before Jay realized what was happening, the hound was wriggling through the pipe.

'You come back here!' Jay threw himself full length on the ground, shoved his arm down the pipe, tried to grab the dog's back legs. But the dog had already clawed his way out the other side. He was inside Prospect, shaking the soil off his coat, looking pleased with himself.

From the top of her tower, Dusk saw the dog. *Wolf's dinner*, she thought.

Jay ran desperately up and down the wire. 'Come back, boy!' Then he stopped dead. He'd seen a way to get in.

A huge oak tree, growing outside the fence, was tilting at a crazy angle, its roots ripped half out of the ground. As it toppled, it had locked branches with another tree, just inside the fence.

I could crawl over there, thought Jay. At the top of both trees, their branches intertwined, made a sort of bridge.

It looked strong enough. And he was light; it would bear his weight. But it was dangerously close to the top of the electric fence. Only about half a metre above it.

'Come back, come back,' Jay begged the dog. It looked at him once, with those big, Bambi eyes, yelped excitedly as if it was saying 'You come in here', and trotted off over the open scrubland towards the town.

Jay pulled his mobile out his pocket, punched in Curtis's number. At least it was ringing. Curtis didn't usually remember to switch it on.

'Come on, come on, come on,' fumed Jay. 'Pick it up.'

'Yeah?' a bleary voice replied.

'Dad!' Jay shouted into the phone. 'Tell me again what you said about Prospect. Did you say there's no radiation?'

Curtis sounded confused. 'No, course there isn't. It was all a big con by the military.'

'You sure?' asked Jay. Before, he'd dismissed what Dad said. Now he wanted to believe it.

'For God's sake, I worked for them, didn't I? They just don't want no one to go snooping around in there.'

'You absolutely *sure* there's no radiation?' It surprised Jay that Curtis was sticking to his story. For once Dad sounded like he knew what he was talking about.

'How many times do I have to tell you? It's safe as houses in there. I seen them go in, when they thought no one was watching, without contamination suits. Where are you anyhow?' added Curtis, like he'd only just thought about it.

But Jay switched off his mobile so Dad couldn't get back to him.

He scrambled, monkey-like, up the tilting trunk of the oak. He even forgot about his craving for his first cigarette.

Curtis had half convinced him about the radiation. But Jay didn't much care one way or the other. He was going into Prospect, whatever. To get his dog back – and, maybe, his self respect.

7

Jay slithered over the tree bridge. The branches were locked together – they felt secure. But they were springy too. Suddenly, the bridge began to sag under his weight, like a hammock.

Awww, no, thought Jay, sweating. Maybe this wasn't such a good idea, after all. The top of the electric fence was right under his belly. He didn't dare move.

But the bridge didn't give any more. He wriggled off it and swung himself down through the tree on the other side.

I'm in! he thought, dropping to the ground. That was easier than he thought. He looked around for his dog.

'Here, boy!'

His voice echoed eerily in the silence. Then he heard a thin, high-pitched whining sound.

Jay looked down. He was waist-deep in a tangle of plants. They had strange flowers, the colour of raw meat, and tall straggly, cone-shaped tubes that reached up to the sun.

From inside the tubes came a frantic buzzing. They were pitcher plants that trapped their prey. All around him was the sound of flies being digested alive. Jay shuddered, pushed his way out of them. He started to walk across the scrubland towards the main street.

The dog appeared from nowhere, started to dance round his heels.

Jay bent down to pat him. 'Hey, dog,' he told it, 'this place is amazing.'

It was a green, jungly ghost town. You could tell it had been abandoned in a hurry. There was a rusty child's bicycle forgotten in the rush to leave . . . even some wisps of washing left on a line.

Dusk's eyes went from wide angle into zoom mode. From her lookout point high in the church tower, she'd been watching the intruder ever since he broke the cover of the trees.

Now they were closer she could see the beads of sweat rolling down his neck; see a red tick crawling about in his dog's ear, looking for a blood vessel to latch on to.

'Go away!' said Dusk fiercely. She couldn't believe he'd dared to come over the fence. He had no right to be here. Prospect belonged to her and Wolf and General Rat.

Jay had no idea he was being watched, no sense of danger. Although he did wonder why, if there was no radioactivity, the military wanted to keep people out. What was there to find here?

I'll ask Dad later, he thought.

But he wasn't worried. His main feeling was excitement, like this was a big adventure. Jay was a lone explorer in a lost and forgotten town. Only, he wasn't alone; he had his faithful hound with him.

Jay pushed his way through some tall purple weeds. He was in Main Street, walking not on tarmac but on cushions of moss. That half collapsed, creeper-smothered building had once been a shop. There was a rusty sign dangling outside that said: J. Huey and Sons.

He scrambled over some briars. A branch whipped out, hooked into his calf.

'Ow.' Jay carefully freed himself. There were trickles of blood running down his leg. The dog sniffed at them. Jay pushed him away.

He glanced inside the store. It was dark in there.

Jay thought about lighting some of his matches, going in, taking a look around. But then he heard scuffling.

Rats? thought Jay. He backed away. Maybe he'd give the store a miss. It hadn't occurred to him there'd be wildlife in Prospect. *Dumb city boy*, he thought, grinning at his own stupidity. *What you expect? It's a wilderness, ain't it?*

And now he began to notice it; there was life all around him. Little yellow birds flickering in bushes. Sparkling blue dragonflies whirring about like mini-helicopters.

The church tower was at the other end of the street, all spun round with ivy, like something out of a fairy tale. He began walking towards it.

Up in the steeple Dusk was getting more and more agitated. He was coming closer. He wasn't going to go away.

As Jay strolled up, a hawk spiralled the top of the tower

and soared off. Dusk saw it fly too. It was the male sparrowhawk, disturbed by the intruder. She followed it with her eyes until it was just a speck in the sky. The female stayed on the nest, but was as twitchy as Dusk. Dusk mewed, to soothe her, but she suddenly shot off, flying after her mate. She wouldn't stay away long, or her eggs would get cold.

'Boy!' yelled Jay again, looking around. 'Here, Boy!'

Up in her hideout, Dusk thought he was making a challenge. Shouting out his name, as if he already owned the place.

Go away, Boy, she thought. He had scared off the hawks – when they belonged here and he didn't.

Jay's trainer crunched on something, right under the tower. He bent down to pick it up.

It was some kind of big, dry pellet, about the size of a shotgun bullet. It seemed to be made mainly of fur. He prodded it. It fell apart on his palm. Jay stared. It was like opening a surprise parcel. Inside it was a jumble of tiny, white bones. He had no idea what they'd make if you fitted them together, like a 3-D jigsaw.

Maybe a mouse, he thought. He puffed the fragile bones off his hand, picked up another pellet. This time he pulled it apart. It had bits of shiny blue beetle wing inside it.

Suddenly he stared up at the tower. Dusk wasn't expecting it. He was directly beneath her. She'd had to lean out of her window, so she could see what he was up to.

There's someone up there! thought Jay.

Dusk knew he'd spotted her. She'd seen the pupils of his

eyes widen in surprise. She hissed defiance but at the same time, she was trembling. If Boy came into the church, started to climb the steeple stairs, she'd be trapped.

She was panicking now. The thought of being helpless, like she had been at SERU, filled her with horror. Dusk saw herself, slumped in her cage, her head lolling . . .

No! she told herself, shuddering at the memory.

Her hand snuck up to the hair slide, tugged at it. When she was lonely, when the hawks were off hunting, she often cleaned it with spit and watched it sparkle. And was surprised all over again that Curtis had given it to her.

No! she told herself, more fiercely than ever. She pulled her hand back, left the hair slide where it was.

Thinking about Curtis's gift only confused her. Dusk didn't need people. She hated them. Even more than the rats.

If Boy came up the stairs she still had an escape route. She could fly away from him.

Suddenly she saw herself, arms and legs spread out, floating and twisting like a winged seed, rising like hawks on warm air currents. As always, the picture entranced her. She clambered on to the window ledge.

Jay stared up at her squatting there, like a frog. His astonished gaze took in her ragged clothes, her lion's mane of white hair, her orange eyes.

It's a girl, he thought. *Is it? What the hell's she doing here?*

She was spreading her skinny arms, tilting forwards to catch the breeze.

She's going to jump! thought Jay. He looked around

for the church door. He had to get up there, stop her.

Dusk didn't seem aware of him. But her hawk eyes were all-seeing. She knew he was heading for the church door.

She closed her eyes; pictured herself flying. It was the only way to stay free.

She's smiling! thought Jay. She wasn't just smiling, she looked blissfully happy. He knew he wasn't going to make it up to the steeple. She tilted even further forwards. The moment seemed frozen in time . . .

'No!' screamed Jay.

Then he heard the howl. He tore his eyes away from Dusk. His head whipped round. More howls came. Whatever creatures made them were hidden in the creeping green jungle. The howls got louder, as if they were moving in.

Dusk heard them too. Her eyes shot open. Her trance was shattered; her flying dream over. She shrieked in anguish. For seconds there, she'd had perfect faith. Believed, with absolute certainty, that she could fly like the hawks.

But the moment had passed. Anyway there was no need now. Boy wasn't a threat. He was as good as dead. Wolf and the dog pack would hunt him down . . .

Wolf and Dusk lived in an uneasy alliance. He hadn't killed her yet, although he could have done every time she left the tower to find food. Dusk didn't think, for one second, it was because she had freed him. And she may have been right about that. There were other reasons for

Wolf to leave Dusk alone. Her ultraviolet vision made her an expert on rat tactics. She could track their glowing trails at night, even in the day, though less clearly. Every splash of urine, every sweaty pawprint they left, betrayed their movements. She knew their rat runs, their nest sites, where they'd been, where they were headed. She could even track General Rat from his extra-large pawprints, see his skull plate glitter from the top of her steeple. And the General was the one both the dogs and Dusk feared most. Without him, the rat hordes would rip each other's throats out. With him in command, they were invincible.

The dogs had learned that Dusk knew the safest places. Where she was, the rats weren't. Often, in return for her own safety, she did the dogs favours. She would guide them to lone rats they could pick off. Other times she screeched alarm calls from the top of her high tower, warning them when the General was manoeuvring his troops.

The dogs weren't all that smart. But even to them, it made more sense to keep the hawk-child alive.

What's going on? thought Jay. He'd only seen small, fluttery wildlife so far. But those howls made the hairs lift on the back of his neck.

Wolf came trotting out from between the houses. Like Dusk, he didn't like people. Except as prey.

He remembered the choke chain biting into his neck when they took him out at SERU to patrol the perimeter fence. He remembered going stir-crazy in his pen, rush-ing at the wire trying to bite his way through. But he still took his time. He knew this human was already dogmeat.

Wolf looked lordly, his head held high. The dogs hunted mostly by day. They were the top predators then. The twilight was Dusk's time. That's when she came down from her high tower. The night belonged to the rats – neither the dogs nor Dusk liked to be about then.

Jay swallowed hard. At first he couldn't believe what he was seeing. He thought frantically, *It's a wolf!'*

His hound dog was scared too. It was yelping hysterically, cringing, its tail jammed between its legs. Suddenly it shot off into the scrubland. Then Jay saw it on the other side of the fence. It had dragged its scrawny body back thought the pipe.

Two thoughts flashed through Jay's brain. One was, *My dog's safe.* And the other was, *That useless dog – it's run out on me!*

Wolf threw the fleeing hound one contemptuous glance. He didn't bother to chase it. He had bigger prey right here, under his nose. He growled at Jay. The grey hair along his spine bristled.

Jesus, thought Jay. *It's going to attack me.'*

He backed off one step at a time, very, very slowly. Then his brain shrieked at him, *Run!* He turned and sprinted for the fence. Wolf didn't choose to chase him either because, when Jay had almost reached the tree that would take him to safety, Wolf's mate and five sons came loping out of the long grass to cut him off.

She was a big husky, pure white with a white ruff round her neck. As soon as Wolf got to Prospect, two years ago, he'd wasted no time finding a mate. When the soldiers came to clear out the townsfolk, the two dogs had kept out of sight. Their first litter produced five sons, two white like her, three black-and-grey like him. But all the time the rats were breeding too, growing more powerful. Wolf and his mate lost their next litter of puppies to the General's army, even before their eyes were open. But still, the seven dogs hunting together made a deadly team.

Jay skidded to a halt, looked around for somewhere else to run.

Wolf's sons waited. While Wolf looked on, their mother moved in first. She was panting, her tongue flopping out, her eyes bright, expectant. She and her family lived mostly on rabbits now. Some pet dogs had been left behind, in the panic to leave the town. But they'd hunted down the last of those long ago.

The church! Jay thought wildly. *I can make it!*

He ran for it, away from the fence towards the church. He thought his heart was going to burst. Jay had almost made it, but Wolf's mate was right behind him, loping easily, not even pushing herself.

Jay yelled as she tore at his leg. She stopped to shake a piece of his shorts out of her teeth. Jay hurled himself into the church.

The door was hanging by one hinge but it would still close. He shoved it shut behind him and fell against it. It wouldn't keep them out long. The church was crumbling. There were holes in every wall where tree roots had smashed their way in.

Jay didn't feel much pain yet. There was too much adrenalin flooding his system. He forced himself up and, dragging his leg, staggered down the weed-choked aisle.

The inside of the church was weirdly peaceful. The last rays of the sun slanted in through the broken windows. Green creepers curled softly over pews and hymn books.

Shivering with shock, Jay prayed, 'Please God, please Jesus.' He was covering his options. Just in case they did exist and Ma had been right all along.

'*Rrrrrrr.*'

He heard a low, rumbling growl somewhere behind him.

Wolf's biggest son was poking a white muzzle through a window. He barked in excitement.

Jay flung himself behind a pew. His leg left a trail of fresh blood behind him.

Wolf's son sniffed the air. He could smell it. He should have hung back. Wolf or his mother should be first in for the kill. But this son was rebellious. It wasn't the first time he'd challenged Wolf's authority.

Jay crawled along behind a pew. His knee bone smacked against an iron ring sticking up from the floor. There was some kind of trapdoor under the ivy.

Feverishly, his hands ripping and tearing, Jay cleared the creepers. Forced up the door, just enough.

Wolf's son burst, in one graceful bound, through a half-broken window, stained glass exploding all around him in a riot of colour and light.

Jay rolled through the gap into darkness. The trapdoor thumped shut. He tumbled helplessly down wooden stairs, cracking his head on the way.

Upstairs, Wolf and his family prowled about, their nostrils still full of the scent of hot blood. While down on the cellar floor, their prey was out cold.

8

Up in the church tower, Dusk was thinking, *Dinner time*.

She scanned Prospect, spread out below her. She had a good view of Main Street from here. The only place she couldn't see was the lily pond, behind the houses, shaded by trees.

She perched on the wide windowsill, hugging her knees. The skin on her arms was smooth. The scratches had healed and, for a long time now, she hadn't felt the need to make any new ones.

Twilight was Dusk's time for hunting. The sparrow-hawks had yellow eyes. They saw best in the day. Night hunters, like owls, had eyes like dark pools. But her orange eyes were for dusk. That eerie, grey, in-between time when reality blurs. She saw best then. That's why scientists at SERU had given her her name.

'General Rat,' called Dusk from the steeple. 'General Rat!' She knew his name from SERU. She'd seen him and the other rats sometimes, when her lab door was left open. Heard the lab assistants talking about them. 'That General. You seen the way he stares at you? That rat gives me the shivers.'

Dusk wouldn't go down until she knew which part of Prospect he and his army were headed for tonight.

Then, it seemed at a given signal, rats swarmed up from their underground nests and burrows. She saw the ground moving, as if it was maggot-ridden. To human eyes, all of the rats, white or brown, would have merged with the grey light. But to Dusk they weren't invisible. Her ultra-violet vision tracked their every move, saw the neon maze of light around them as they raced along their rat highways. Even where a scaly tail had looped round a twig, she saw the mark, like a golden wedding ring.

'There!' said Dusk.

At the head of the rat mob she saw the General. She saw the silver plate glint in his skull, picked up his bigger footprints.

They were going towards the rabbit hill on the far side of town.

Dusk nodded, pleased. She knew now where she would hunt. It would be far away from them.

She didn't need to worry about Wolf. He and his family were holed up for the night. Their den was the empty vault under the Prospect bank. Even the rats couldn't gnaw their way through those steel walls.

Dusk didn't worry about Boy either. She hadn't seen the kill. But he'd been hunted down by Wolf's strongest son. She just assumed he was dead by now. And the dog pack would be sleeping, with fat bellies.

Satisfied that it was safe to go down, Dusk hopped from the window ledge back into the steeple.

They used to cut her toenails and fingernails at SERU.

It made it harder for her to self harm. It also made it harder for her to rake people's eyes. Like a hawk surprised on the ground by a big predator, a cat or fox, Dusk always went for the eyes first.

The first time she tried it she was very small. SERU brought in a psychologist – a child expert – to try to socialize her. Perhaps they even thought she could mix with other kids one day. The child expert didn't last long. She taught Dusk some social skills – toilet trained her, and taught her the names of things from baby books. Then one day, the woman made a big mistake. She'd snuck up behind Dusk, put her hands over her eyes, said, 'Dusk. Guess who's here?' Blinded, Dusk had gone berserk. She'd missed the woman's eyes, but raked open her face from forehead to chin.

'Socialize her?' the child expert had screamed, trying to staunch the blood with some tissues. 'She's a little savage! Sedate her!'

They used to cut Dusk's nails when she was drugged up – she would have fought like a tiger otherwise. But now her nails were long, dirty talons. She liked them that way.

But she needed other weapons too.

Dusk could target her prey like a hawk, pick out a scuttling cockroach in poor light. Although she only ate them when hunting was poor. But when her hawk eyes had homed in on dinner, what did she do then? She couldn't swoop down and trap it under outspread wings. Her nails broke if she tried to skewer it. Dusk had been lucky with that first mouse. After that, most of her meals got away. Some days when she first came to Prospect she'd almost starved. She had to dig in the soil for worms and millipedes.

At first she'd gone wild with frustration, scratched herself until she bled whenever she missed her prey. Hunger gnawed at her, like a monster tearing her belly. Dusk longed for her cage back at SERU, for the comforting 'Ping!' of the microwave. At least there she'd never been hungry. She even longed for people in white coats to look after her.

They didn't come. She was close to giving in. Just closing her eyes, curling up on the floor and dying, like a sick animal. But her human brain, made drowsy for so long by drugs, refused to let her die in peace. It pestered her: *You can stay alive. I can show you ways.*

It drove her down from the steeple. Sent her scavenging in the houses. She didn't stay long because the houses weren't safe. Some were collapsing. But the main danger was they were rat territory. You could hear them scuffling under the floorboards, behind the walls. But the people of Prospect, harassed by the military, had left possessions behind. Dusk had taken some, experimented.

She'd found a string bag, made it into a throwing net. Weighted it with pebbles. She'd found a two-pronged pitchfork with a long handle and practised using them together – throw, stab, throw, stab. At first it was hit and miss. Some days she still ate worms and millipedes. But she'd got better at it. These days her prey still escaped – but only maybe one out of three.

Those first desperate days in Prospect seemed far away. Now Dusk had learned to fend for herself, live by her own wits. She buckled a thick man's leather belt round her skinny waist. She'd found that in a house, too. She tucked her throwing net into it, picked up her pitchfork.

Dusk pictured a snake in her head. 'No!' she warned herself, grinning.

She could smile now. But that mistake, in her first months in Prospect, had nearly killed her. She'd seen a shimmer of coils. Throw, stab. But she'd fumbled with the pitchfork. The rattler had bitten her ankle. For days she'd lain sick in the steeple, sweating, shivering, passing in and out of consciousness.

Now Dusk kept well away from rattlers.

In spring she took starling chicks right out of the nest. She could have taken the sparrowhawk's chicks too. Just leaned out the window and grabbed them for an easy snack. But that was taboo. She felt a natural bond with hawks. They were like family.

Rat babies for dinner, decided Dusk, smacking her lips.

Rat babies weren't off the menu. Rats were enemies. They would kill her instantly if they caught her. And their babies were plentiful, born all year round. Taking them wasn't without risks. But, as long as she knew where the rat army was, she was safe.

There was a plastic bottle in the corner. Dusk stored her water here, for the daytime when she rarely left the steeple. She took a long pull from the bottle.

She didn't fill it from the pond. Dusk avoided that place. There was something hidden in the water – something big that made the lily pads shiver. She got her water

80

from an underground spring that bubbled up by the church. Dusk didn't know it was supposed to be radio-active; she couldn't read the signs.

In the steeple, Dusk had other things she'd brought back from her looting trips. She had a heap of clothes. At first she'd worn the T-shirt and shorts she escaped in from SERU. They'd grown ragged, stiff with blood and sweat. So she went out to find some more. Plenty of clothes had been forgotten, left behind in drawers and laundry baskets. Dusk found some T-shirts with glittery words on them. She had no idea what they said. She just loved anything that sparkled.

Before she padded down the steeple steps, Dusk did one more thing. She'd found a shiny steel comb in one of the houses. Dusk dragged it through her hair, like Curtis showed her. Took out her hair slide, polished it, put it back. Thinking about Curtis's kindness wasn't a threat now. It wouldn't weaken her – make her wonder if perhaps Boy wasn't all bad. Because Boy was safely dead.

Dusk was ready to go out hunting. *You look real pretty*, she told herself. She padded down into the church.

She saw Boy's blood spotting the ivy leaves. It didn't surprise her there was no body. The dogs had dragged it off somewhere to feed in private. She dismissed Boy from her mind. He hadn't really been a danger. Dusk had seen straightaway that he didn't have her power, was as help-less in Prospect as rat babies or puppies. She might have felt sorry for him, if she didn't hate people so much.

*

81

Long before Dusk went out hunting, Jay had come round, down in the cellar.

He lay for a long time in the dark, trying to work out what had happened. He remembered his mind exploding into a brilliant white starburst, then darkness. He remembered his own hound escaping. Then the dogs hunting him down; that big white one taking a piece out of his leg.

Cautiously, in the dark, he felt for the bite, just above his knee.

'Ow!' he cried out when he found it. It hurt like crazy. He had no idea what to do about it. Ma would have known. She was good when you hurt yourself. Jay thought vaguely, *If it's bleeding, it needs a tourniquet or something.* He'd seen them do that in films. He felt again, trying to be gentle, but the blood was dried up, crusty. At least he wasn't about to bleed to death.

Now his brain was working better, he thought, *Where did those dogs come from?*

Were they pets gone wild? Guard dogs or something, left behind by the military?

He stopped thinking about that. The main thing was to get out of here. What if the dogs were waiting outside? He thought, *Call Dad on your mobile.* Why hadn't he thought of that before? Then he decided, *No, call Ma.* She was five hundred miles away but you could depend on her in a crisis. Curtis would say, 'Just let me grab another beer. Then I'll do something.'

Jay felt in his pocket of his shorts for his mobile; couldn't find it. It must have slipped out as he fell. He crawled around groping for it.

His fingers gripped plastic. *Got it!* he thought, feeling a rush of hope. Now he was in contact with the outside world.

Then he felt wires, sharp edges, and he realized his fingers were in the guts of the phone. It was smashed, unusable. Disgusted, he hurled it into the dark. Heard it clatter off a wall somewhere.

'Useless piece of junk!'

He was almost crying with frustration. Moving so fast had made him want to throw up. He'd forgotten about hitting his head. Now it felt like a stormy sea was crashing inside it.

He stayed very still until the nausea passed. Ages seemed to drift by. Jay wished he had something to smoke. He thought, *No one knows I'm here.*

Then he remembered about the girl. The weird-looking one he'd seen in the steeple window. Her white hair had made her look spectral, like a ghost child. But her vivid orange eyes had burned with life.

'She was going to throw herself out that window,' he marvelled. 'But she was smiling!'

Was she real? He wasn't sure now. Maybe he'd dreamed her up when he was out cold. But his fantasy girls weren't anything like that. They were sexy, of course, but they were sweet at the same time. The kind of girls you could talk to, who would appreciate your company. Who wouldn't say, 'Get lost, creep!' and giggle about you with their friends. He hadn't found a real girl like that yet. He stopped looking since the fight with Little Shane, scared no girls would want to be seen with him.

But if he had been looking, the girl in the window would have been his date from hell. Everything about her said 'Hands off!' She seemed fierce, unapproachable. A wild-looking freak.

More time passed.

Jay told himself, *You gotta do something. You can't just stay here.* Nobody was coming to save him. Even his dog had run out on him.

Tears of despair sprang to his eyes. He could die in this cellar and nobody would know. He dashed the tears away with a fist. Made his lip stop quivering, got his emotions under control.

What you doing, waiting for Jesus to save you? he mocked himself.

Since he got beat up, he'd been like his own policeman. Accusing himself all the time. Not letting himself get away with anything. Watching for the least weakness.

'Move it!' he ordered himself out loud, like a sergeant of marines.

But secretly, a little voice inside was begging, *Just don't fall apart. Right? Like you did after the fight.*

Jay started to drag himself up the cellar steps. He found his cap halfway up. Fitted it, very gently, back on his head.

Least my brains won't fall out, he told himself.

He was pleased that he'd managed to make a joke. Even a feeble one. It showed he wasn't going to pieces. Maybe he could trust himself a bit more. Maybe he was going to get out of this OK.

Wouldn't it be great if his friends knew about it?

Said, 'Wow! And you didn't, like, panic? I would've been shitting myself!'

He felt that, after what happened with Little Shane, he had to redeem himself somehow. Maybe Prospect was his big chance.

With both hands, he pushed up the trapdoor and peered through.

He couldn't see much, mainly creepers. He listened. No savage howls. The church felt peaceful in the grey gloom. It was later than he thought. The stillness of the evening had settled over it. But it seemed like it was safe to go out. He decided to risk it.

Jay slid out of the cellar. He tested his bad leg. Hauled himself up on a pew.

It hurt. But at least he could walk on it.

He was heading for the church door when he heard barking. It was in the distance but he thought, *They're still out there*. He remembered how Wolf's son had burst through the stained-glass window.

Jay felt flutterings of panic. But he tried to think. There was only one place to retreat to. He looked around. How did you get up to the steeple? He'd rather face the freak than the dogs.

He hobbled over moss and grass to a narrow door behind the preacher's pulpit. It wasn't choked with ivy. It looked like someone used it, regularly.

He prayed, *Please God, don't let it be locked*.

It was a heavy door, the kind you couldn't smash down. It was criss-crossed with iron bands, had a big, iron ring for a handle. He turned the ring, held his breath. The door opened.

Jay listened at the bottom of the steep, narrow steps. He couldn't hear anything. 'Hello,' he called. No reply. Jay stood at the bottom undecided. He had no idea what was waiting for him up there. Then he heard the dogs bark again, this time closer. He shuddered. He didn't have a choice.

Limping, Jay went through the door, latched it behind him.

How long has she been in Prospect? he asked himself, as he struggled up the stairs. *Not long*, he reasoned. She couldn't have survived on her own, without anyone to help her. She was lucky those wild dogs hadn't got her already.

He reached the last step. The little square room at the top of the tower was empty. Dusk was out hunting.

Where is she? thought Jay, looking round wildly. He thought again, *Maybe I dreamed her.*

He limped over to the window, looked down at Prospect. It wasn't fully dark yet. But from this height he couldn't make out anything clearly. The green jungle, the collapsing buildings, had all melted into spooky shadows.

His head had started to swim again. It was no good; he had to sit down. Gently, Jay let himself down to the floor. Closed his eyes.

Then the smell hit him. His eyes shot open. *It stinks in here!*

Jay looked around. Found where the smell came from. There was dried blood, bits of fur – even feathers – all over the place. He looked closer.

Gross, he thought, feeling sick. There were beaks among the stinking mess and scaly clawed feet. He was sitting in them.

Shuffling sideways to a cleaner bit of floor, he almost knocked over Dusk's water supply. Piled next to it was her little stash of treasures. Like a magpie's hoard, it all sparkled: some spectacles, a broken gold watch, the T-shirts, a silver comb – other things she'd salvaged from the crumbling houses. So the girl was real, after all.

It looked like she'd been living here quite a while. *Glad she's not here*, he thought. What kind of girl combed her hair, wore cute, sparkly T-shirts but lived among decaying animal corpses?

He had to think of a way to get out of Prospect before she came back. Jay really, really didn't want to meet her. Those dogs alone were more trouble than he needed.

But he couldn't think about getting out right now. His head ached too much. He tried to swallow and couldn't find any spit. His throat felt as if it was packed with ashes.

Jay unscrewed the top of Dusk's water bottle. He had to have a drink. A little warning voice said, *What if Curtis isn't right? What if it's radioactive?*

But he just didn't care. He took a long swig then told himself, *You better clean that bite.*

The water made the wound burn like fire. The pain made him weak and shivery.

Hope my dog finds someone to feed it, he thought. Jay leaned his head against the wall, closed his eyes.

He'd redeem himself, after a little rest.

9

While Jay slept in the steeple, Dusk was hunting for her dinner.

With her throwing net and pitchfork she could have been a Roman girl gladiator brought back to life. Except for the trashy plastic hair slide, the T-shirt that said *ANGEL* across the front in gold glitter. And those brilliant orange eyes that betrayed her as not quite one hundred per cent human.

Everywhere she walked she could see rodent tracks. To her, Prospect wasn't lost in hazy grey light. It was alive with glowing yellow trails, splashes, smears. Some were faint – they were made hours ago. But some were fresh. They lit up the ground like neon signs.

Dusk's ultraviolet vision picked up a golden dribble. A grass stem right beside it quivered. The mouse that had sprinkled its pee all around had taken cover, thinking it was safe.

Dusk grinned, wide and confidently, like someone at ease with herself, happy in her own skin. She knew she was good at this. Dusk was proud of her hunting skills. Her hand crept to her throwing net. She flung it expertly.

Frisbee-like, it spun through the air. Flopped down on the startled rodent. Dusk sprang forwards, ready to stab. She didn't have to. Like most small mammals she hunted, the mouse was already dead of heart failure.

Usually she took her prey back to the steeple to eat it. But this evening she was too hungry.

Dusk untangled the mouse from her throwing net. Held up the still-warm, furry body by the tail. Opened her mouth, slid it in.

Then she reminded herself sternly, *Rat babies*. They were the tastiest treat and, if you were careful, easy to take.

She had to get to the nests before the General returned with his rat hordes. The rats were very dangerous. No alliances, like the one she had with Wolf, were possible with them.

Rats came swarming over the ground like a grey sea. They attacked anything alive in their way. Like soldier ants, they could leave a corpse stripped bare. Rats usually live off the garbage humans produce. But apart from Dusk, there were no people left in Prospect. So these rats didn't scavenge, they killed. It was in their genes anyway. The scientists at SERU had bred them like that and, this time, the experiment had been a big success.

All the General had to do was control them. Keep them from killing each other, or him. He was always surrounded by a bodyguard of his loyal offspring. They executed any rat that disobeyed him. They drove the old ones, who were no more use, out into the wilderness. That's where Dusk and the dogs picked them off. But the

General didn't have too much trouble with his troops. They were very dumb – as long as he gave them enough things to kill they were satisfied. And their numbers just kept growing and growing. Which was just what the General wanted. He wasn't content to rule Prospect. He was a rat with ambition.

'*Shhhh*, quiet,' Dusk warned herself, putting a finger to her lips. Since she'd escaped from SERU, Dusk had discovered a sense of humour. She often joked with herself while out hunting. Teased herself, in a friendly way. 'Dusk, you will get no dinner. You are making too much noise.' That was something her carers back at SERU used to say to her.

Dusk trod softly down the main street of Prospect. She was heading for J. Huey and Sons. She didn't like hunting inside buildings but she knew there were nests there, full of squirming rat babies.

In the evening, when they went out hunting, the rats left their nests undefended, save for a few female lookouts. If they saw Dusk they would squeal out warnings. Sometimes the General was too far away to hear. Sometimes he wasn't and then Dusk had to move very fast. Once, when her hair slide fell out and she went back to find it, he'd almost caught her. She'd only got back to the steeple by the skin of her teeth.

The store was slap-bang in the middle of a maze of rat runs. From high up they looked like a giant, luminous cat's cradle. It was the General's HQ and their main nesting site. Dusk could spy on them from her tower. The rats could do most things. Squeeze like toothpaste through tiny spaces, gnaw through aluminium sheets, even swim – but they weren't natural climbers. Dusk felt safe up in the steeple. But down here it was their territory. You had to stay alert. Use all your senses.

Dusk wrinkled her nose. '*Ssssss.*' She hissed in disgust. You could smell it even outside – the rats' strong, musky stink.

She put a hand to her belt, just to reassure herself her throwing net was still there. Dusk gripped her pitchfork lightly. She pushed her way through a tangle of tall, yellow daisies to the door of the rats' HQ. Caught her foot in a loop of bramble. When she freed herself, a row of tiny red beads spurted up where the thorns had punctured her skin.

'Shit!' said Dusk. That was something else she'd heard Curtis say. She didn't know what it meant. She used it, like he had, as an exclamation of pain.

Dusk frowned. It wasn't good to have the smell of fresh blood on you. It made it easy for the rats to sniff you out.

She stood undecided, weighing up the risks. But the lure of rat babies was too strong. Dusk stepped inside the store. Stood for a moment to get her bearings in the musty-smelling gloom. In here the rat trails, faint and fresh, were like tangled string, too complex to make sense of.

She heard scuffling sounds. Were they coming from under the floor boards? Her predator eyes blazed bright orange. They zoomed in on movement. She saw shaggy brown fur, a pink naked tail, whiskers. It was a female rat. She'd smelled Dusk before she'd seen her. The rat was already streaking outside to call the General back.

Dusk told herself, *Run away!*

Then she found the nests. It was the General's soldier factory. Great smelly heaps of old rags and paper with rat babies wriggling in the middle like giant, pink maggots.

Dusk licked her lips.

But she was being attacked. Something landed on her head. Instinctively, her third eyelids slid across to protect her vision.

She gave a hiss of anger. '*Ssss!*' The rat scrabbled in her hair. Impatiently, she knocked it off. She preferred tender babies to stringy old females.

Now more females left on guard were squealing They stood up on their hind legs. Their eyes glowed red, like twin lasers in the gloom. The one outside was sending shrill, high-pitched alarm calls into the evening air.

Quick, quick, Dusk said to herself. Her hawk language was fluent. She used it every day. Dusk could mimic every hawk call, knew all their meanings, but her human speech was rusty after two years. Talking to herself was the only practice she got.

Run fast! She'd cut it very fine. She thought she'd have more time.

Dusk snatched a couple of rat babies. She didn't even need to use her pitchfork – just snapped their necks between her finger and thumb. Tucked them by the tails into her belt. Turned to run.

Outside, evening was darkening into night. Already a big silver moon hung in the sky. Dusk preferred it cloudier than this. That's when her eyes worked best.

But it was time to go home.

General Rat was on his way back. Was she already cut off? Dusk stuck her pitchfork in the ground, climbed like a cat up the nearest tree.

Her hawk eyes could see them. A seething mass of rat bodies, all rushing in this direction. She saw a flash of silver. It was the General's skull plate, glinting in the moonlight. The General ran with his bodyguards round him. A few were white, like him. Most had white-flecked fur. They would defend the General to the death.

Dusk slid down the tree, scraping skin off her legs. She snatched her pitchfork and ran. Adrenalin pumped through her body. She was afraid of the rats; only a fool wouldn't be. But it gave her a buzz to outwit them. It made her feel the man who'd given her the present had been right. She chanted his words to herself she ran. 'You know what? You're clever, Dusk.'

She could feel the ground shake now. Dusk spun round, looked back through the gap between the houses. Main Street was alive – a stormy sea, seething with a torrent of running rats, hundreds of them.

It was a deadly game she was playing. Even for her, she was cutting it fine. She'd seen it from her tower, how the rats engulfed their victims. Left nothing behind but scraps of bloodied bone. The rats didn't seem to feel pain or fear. They knew no danger. They didn't need allies. They would do anything the General ordered.

Even face certain death.

Dusk had seen one do that once, when she was out hunting. It was doggy-paddling across the waterlily pond. The General had sent it on a suicide mission. He was curious to find out what lurked under the lily pads. But whatever it was never surfaced. Just snatched the rat's legs from below and pulled him down, in a swirl of water.

Panting hard, Dusk reached the church. She found a hole in the wall, an alternative entrance. Squeezed through the ivy into the moonwashed nave.

She swivelled her head, looked around.

There was an eerie stillness in the church, like the eye of a storm. Gauzy moonlight made it look magical, silvered even the spikiest thorns. For a few seconds Dusk drank it in – that healing tranquillity. Her thumping heart slowed.

'Home,' she said.

But she wasn't safe yet. She vaulted over a pew. Then another. As she flew through the air, the word ANGEL on her T-shirt shimmered.

At the door to the steeple, she glanced back. The rats weren't behind her. But it had been a very close call. She made sure the steeple door was shut tight behind her, raced up the steps.

She leaped up on the window ledge, squatting there like a frog. The sparrowhawk had come back to her nest. Dusk mewed a greeting. The hawk stirred, fluffed up her feathers. Then settled down again. Dusk knew the male would be keeping watch nearby. Now Boy was gone, everything was back to normal. It was just her and the hawks.

Dusk coughed a couple of times, as if she was going to be sick. Leaned forwards. A pellet popped out of her mouth, dropped through space to the ground below. It was the bones and fur of the mouse she'd caught. Its indigestible remains, got rid of in a neat little parcel.

She scanned Prospect, looking for rats. Instantly she picked out their freshest tracks. A wide, glowing river of luminous light led straight to their HQ. They weren't even coming this way.

'Good,' said Dusk, nodding to herself.

She jumped down from her ledge to get a swallow of water. It was only then that she saw Jay. She'd have seen him straightaway if he'd been moving. But he was slumped against the wall, still asleep, his mouth open.

'Boy!' said Dusk, shocked and astonished. She'd thought the dogs would be gnawing his bones.

Down on Main Street, the General let his troops stream by him, back into the rats' HQ. He stayed outside for a moment, surrounded by his personal bodyguards. He sniffed the ground. Thrust his blunt muzzle into the earth. He smelled blood.

He knew it was Dusk's. Her smell was very familiar to him. It wasn't the first time she'd come robbing nests, taking his soldiers. She was good at staying alive. She seemed able to predict his every movement. But the General was patient. Dusk had skills other humans didn't have. So far they'd helped her to survive. But her smell told him she *was* human, just like Curtis, the lab assistant. So he knew, one day, she would make a mistake.

He twitched his whiskers. There was another smell here, besides Dusk's. Another human. And it was quite fresh. He sniffed again at Jay's blood, sprinkled on the ground where the briar had scratched him. Maybe this one would be easier to catch. The General was pleased.

His rat army had started off with only a few troops, the ones he'd led to safety at SERU. Now he had hundreds at his command. They had practised on rabbits and feral cats and puppies long enough. It was time to try them out on humans. He would lose some along the way, maybe hundreds. But he expected that; in fact it was part of his plan. Soldiers are expendable. And every day, the female rats gave birth to fresh supplies.

Up in the steeple, Dusk gave hawk cries of rage and alarm. She grasped her pitchfork.

'Mine!' she said. She meant, 'This is my place.'

For two years Dusk had guarded it fiercely. No rats or dogs had ever been up here. No humans either, after the search party. She didn't share it with anyone, except hawks.

'Go away!' she told the intruder.

He didn't respond.

Dusk stalked up to him, warily, pitchfork ready to strike. She saw blood on his leg, in crusty ridges on his face. Maybe he was dead. He looked dead.

She lowered her pitchfork. Put her head on one side, inspected him. The Japanese character on his cap glittered in the moonlight. Dusk's hawk eyes stared, spellbound. She wanted that cap. She put out a hand to snatch it. Before she could, Jay moaned. Dusk jumped back. He was alive! Dusk screeched a protest. Jumped on a wooden bench, swung herself up into the beams. She didn't need to fly. He was injured; she could kill him. And she killed best from above.

Deep in his troubled sleep, where Little Shane was

pounding his face to pulp, Jay heard Dusk screeching. He struggled to open his eyes. Make sense of his surroundings. The first thing he saw was the glittering word *ANGEL*. He gazed at it, half awake, uncomprehending. It shifted from moonlight into shadow and back again as Dusk moved about.

'Angel,' he murmured to himself, enchanted. She was all sparkly. Something in her hair was sparkling too.

Dusk screeched again. This time, Jay's eyes shot open. He was wide awake now. It wasn't an angel crouched above him, but what looked like a savage. The girl had come back.

His shocked gaze took in her shaggy blonde hair, her crazy orange eyes and the dead rats dangling from her belt. Her eyes weren't softened with pity, like an angel's should be. They blazed with fierce intensity. There was something wild and primitive about them. As if she came from a time before humans, before angels, before religions.

The transparent membranes slid across Dusk's eyes. They always shielded her sight when she was going to make a kill.

'It's OK,' Jay managed to say. 'I'm not going to hurt you.'

Then his eyes focused on the twin prongs of the pitchfork she was holding. And he knew that she meant to hurt him.

Redeeming himself went right out the window. He tried to roll out of the way. Dusk didn't move. She was used to her prey taking evasive measures. And this one was really slow and clumsy.

She shifted her pitchfork very slightly so it was aimed at the back of his neck, where his spinal cord met his skull. If she jabbed there, it would paralyse him.

Jay twisted his head round. *Jesus!* he thought. He held his hands out, palms downwards and patted the air, in sign language that said, 'Hey, let's cool this down, shall we?' Jay didn't know it, but it was a gesture learned from Curtis years ago, when Jay was small and copied everything Curtis did and wanted to grow up just like his dad.

Dusk followed every movement of his hands, her hawk eyes bright, attentive. Something clicked in her brain when he made that calming gesture. But she still held the pitchfork rock-steady.

Jay stopped trying to pacify her. It didn't seem to be working. *Run!* his brain screamed at him. But where would he go? What about the dogs?

He tried struggling to his feet. His leg wouldn't hold him. He collapsed, started dragging himself through the decaying animals' remains to the door. Jay knew he wasn't going to be quick enough. Something instinctive took over. He stopped moving, lay very, very still.

Jay didn't know it, but some of Dusk's prey escaped like that. By freezing, still as stone. It was mostly when they moved that she attacked.

But it wasn't that that saved his life. It was because he'd reminded Dusk of Curtis, brought all her confused longings flooding back. Dusk was struggling inside, her human needs overriding her hawk instincts. She gripped the pitchfork tighter. Hesitated, only for a few seconds. But it was too long. In those crucial moments between seeing and killing, doubts had entered her mind. Now she couldn't do it.

Jay heard Dusk shriek at herself in anger and disgust. Then, nothing.

He lay still, trying to stop his muscles twitching. One in his cheek was still pulsing, like a tiny heartbeat. Every second he expected to hear Dusk shriek again and feel the pitchfork. Still nothing happened. Except for the blood whooshing in his ears, it was totally silent in the steeple.

Jay's head was turned sideways, away from Dusk. Silver moonlight spilled on to the floor just by his face. Traced a delicate pattern, like lace. Time seemed suspended. He watched the shifting light, fascinated.

Then his brain took over. *See what she's doing*, it ordered him.

He turned his head very, very carefully.

Jay hadn't heard her move. But she wasn't up in the beams. She was sitting hunched in the steeple window, with her back to him. Her pitchfork was on the ledge beside her. But she wasn't holding it.

Dusk was leaning forwards, letting the night air stroke her cheek, soft as velvet. Her orange eyes were closed. That blissful smile transformed her fierce face. She looked girl-like to Jay, and vulnerable. Not dangerous any more. The blue plastic hair slide sparkled in her hair.

She spread out her arms, like wings. It was just like before. *She's going to jump*, Jay thought. *Let her*, he told himself. She'd just tried to stab him. But she hadn't actually *done* it, had she? Something had stopped her.

'Don't jump!' screamed Jay.

99

She didn't even turn round. Dusk was in a trance, totally focused on flying. She wasn't just trying to escape from him. She was trying to escape from her own human emotions. For the first time, they'd made her botch a kill. That's very bad news, if you pride yourself on being one of Prospect's top predators.

Jay hurled himself at the window. As he reached her, she let herself fall. He grabbed her round the waist. She shrieked, that high-pitched, bird of prey screech that did his head in. He hauled her back in, using all his strength. Her pitchfork went clattering out of the window. Dusk fell on top of him on the steeple floor among the claws and scaly feet. She was scratching at his eyes, twisting, kicking.

Jay thought, *I can't keep hold of her.*

Then she suddenly went limp, pretending to be dead.

Jay crawled out from under her, panting. Suddenly, his rage was much stronger than his fear.

'Don't you ever . . .' he shouted at her, furiously. 'Don't you *ever* try that again!'

10

In the late afternoon, Curtis was sitting on his front porch sipping beer, swatting the flies away.

He'd read Jay's note. Curtis expected him to be back long before this. Jay had only been to the store at the turn-off. *Where is that boy?* Curtis was thinking. *What's he getting up to?* He didn't worry too much. Jay's Ma did enough worrying for both of them. He thought, *The boy's probably enjoying some freedom. Not being preached at every minute.* He told himself, *You should call his mobile.*

But he didn't want Jay to think he was checking up on him. *Boy his age needs some independence*, he thought. *Don't want his parents breathing down his neck all the time.*

Curtis chuckled to think what he'd been getting up to at Jay's age.

All the same, it was getting late. The boy had been gone for hours. As Curtis opened another can, he shifted uneasily in his chair. Jay's Ma would play war if he got into any trouble. And Curtis knew he was a careless dad, a bad example. He hardly knew his son at all. He'd left bringing him up to his Ma.

She's better at it, thought Curtis. *God knows how he'd have turned out if he was around me all the time.*

He did wonder, briefly, why Jay had called up, asking about Prospect. He'd only been half awake at the time. The boy was probably roaming around, happened to be passing, saw the signs.

He can't get in, Curtis reassured himself. The electric fence kept everyone out. Anyway, why would he want to? It was like a jungle in there. There was nothing to see. Just a town almost swallowed up by wilderness. Soon you wouldn't know Prospect had ever existed.

The military had searched Prospect several times after the fire at SERU. They'd searched the surrounding woods. Curtis couldn't understand that. Unless they were looking for Dusk. That meant they hadn't recaptured her. Or found any trace of her body in the burned-out buildings.

Did she really escape? Curtis asked himself for the hundredth time.

Even if she did, there was no way she would have lasted long in the forest. She was as helpless as a kitten. *Not a kitten*, Curtis corrected himself. No one would call Dusk cute. Maybe a tiger cub was more like her. Anyhow, it was obvious she couldn't take care of herself.

But if the army suspected she'd survived, even for a few days, they'd move heaven and earth to stop anyone finding her. Like evacuate a whole town, just in case she was hiding out there. Even her bones mustn't be found. That's why Prospect had to stay sealed off. One bone fragment, one tooth, one hair, just a trace of her DNA, would prove what they'd done to her.

And what they'd done to her, if it ever went public, would be dynamite.

The computer disk Curtis took had told him some of it. Scientists had cloned hawks' eye genes, put them in mice before. But no one had ever done it to a human embryo. Until Dusk.

Dusk had hawk and human genes – she was transgenic. It was an illegal, highly unethical experiment.

Not that those military bastards cared about that, thought Curtis, wiping beer froth off his face.

After the fire, the military had paid Curtis a visit. They were suspicious. They didn't mention Dusk. But they asked where he'd been when the fire broke out.

He'd lied, told them he'd been in a different lab. They left after a while. But he wasn't sure if they were convinced. They must have seen they'd made him nervous, that he was sweating like a pig.

He thought about Dusk often. After the fire, when the pain from his burns kicked in, she'd wanted to comfort him. He'd swear to that. Her hawk eyes were cruel. But when he gave her that hair slide, she'd behaved like any kid at Christmas. He could remember her cries of delight. Afterwards, he'd seen a card of plastic hair slides at the store. Lied when he'd bought one, 'It's for my brother's little kid.' Curtis didn't have a brother. It was for Dusk, if he ever met her again. He mocked himself afterwards. 'What did you buy that for? You know she's dead, don't you?'

But he'd kept it at the bottom of a drawer, just in case.

Little freak had human feelings, thought Curtis. All you had to do was treat her decent. But to the military, she was just an experiment to make better soldiers.

'For My Country's Defence!' said Curtis, raising his beer can in a drunken mock salute.

He raised it in another salute, a heartfelt one this time, to Dusk. 'To you, little hell cat,' he said, 'wherever you are.'

Up in the steeple, Jay was totally confused. He'd just saved the girl's life. That was a cool thing to do – he was quite proud of himself. But she didn't seem grateful.

Least she's not trying to stab me or anything, thought Jay. She couldn't; her pitchfork had fallen out of the window.

Dusk could see it now, stuck in the ivy, halfway down the tower. It hadn't fallen far. But it was still way out of reach.

She was sitting, like before, hunched in the window. Looking down on the moonlit town, checking the rats' activities, like she did every night. She'd failed to kill Jay. He'd stopped her flying away. So, with her escape options closed down, she was trying to pretend he didn't exist.

Without taking her brilliant orange eyes off Prospect, she took a rat baby off her belt, held it up by the tail, opened her mouth wide and dropped it in.

Jay couldn't believe what he'd just seen. 'What the . . .?' Then she did it again, just as casually.

His eyes still wide with shock, he told himself, *Get out of here! Get back to the real world*. This was like

104

being stuck in a horror film. He kept thinking, *This can't be happening*.

He limped towards the stairs, desperately trying to be stealthy. Not make any sudden moves that would make her look round.

Dusk tried to ignore him. But her hawk eyes wouldn't let her. They just couldn't help tracking his movements, locking on to that cap logo that glinted in the shadows.

She thought, *Good*. Boy was going away. Leaving the steeple. The rats would get rid of him for her. Then she could finally forget him and the way he'd messed up her mind. She swivelled her head back to the window, pretending she hadn't seen him.

Why was he creeping anyway? Did Boy really think she was going to stop him going?

Jay stopped at the top of the steps, stared down them. He was desperate to get out of here. But he was torn in two. Was it safer in here with her? Or outside? The thought of the dog pack haunted him. The white one bursting through the stained-glass window . . .

He looked back at Dusk. He suddenly needed to ask her things; like, *Do you think those dogs will be out there?* He needed some reassurance. But her back was to him, stiff, unyielding.

Dusk was concentrating, scanning the town. To her, Prospect wasn't abandoned. It teemed with life. It was a dazzle of moving lights, like a busy twenty-four-hour city. But something was bothering her. The rats were moving about a lot tonight. She didn't like the look of that.

Where are you, General Rat? she was thinking.

Jay thought, *What's going on in her head?*

He had no idea how to communicate with her. Even with normal girls it was a minefield. You were scared of making mistakes. Never sure you were doing the right thing. But there were some rules to help you. How you spoke, what you did. But with this girl, the rule book didn't apply. You had to forget anything you'd ever learned.

He thought, *That's cos she's some kind of mutant.* He'd heard there were kids like that, in the backwoods, hidden away from the world. Maybe her family had abandoned her. Or she'd run away, gone feral. Maybe she was brain damaged in some way. Her eyes seemed bright with intelligence but he hadn't once heard her speak. Just screech, like a wild animal.

He limped up to her. 'Excuse me,' he said. He didn't know why he was being so polite, like she was a normal person. She ate rats for God's sake. And she smelled. Not that Jay could be critical about that. He thought, *You caught a whiff of yourself lately?* He smelled rancid too, of sweat and dried blood.

There was no response. *Like talking to a brick wall*, thought Jay.

'Look,' he said. 'You deaf or something? Will those dogs be around if I go outside? I really need to know!'

He stretched out a hand. He meant to grab her shoulder, turn her round, make her look at him. Like she could read his mind, Dusk screeched out a warning. Then screeched again, furious that he'd made her acknowledge him.

Jay jumped back. 'Do you have to make that noise?'

No answer. She hadn't even turned round. Jay gave up. Better to take his chances outside in the wilderness than be stuck in here, with some mutant freak.

'I'm going then,' he said.

So why didn't he do it? He looked back at her one last time. When she had her back to you, you couldn't see her orange eyes. You could kid yourself there was nothing wrong with her.

He thought, *I can't leave her behind. I just can't.* In this savage place, all alone. He was amazed he felt that way. She was crazy; she tried to attack people. But she'd calmed down now. And anyone could see it wasn't her fault, how she acted. Maybe, when they got out of here, she could get help. Doctors, therapists, *somebody*.

'You coming with me?' Jay asked.

For the first time, Dusk spoke to him. She said, 'Go away!'

So she could talk then. That made Jay even more reluctant to leave without her. Besides, he was trying to redeem himself, after Little Shane stole his self respect. He'd couldn't just slink away, leave her here to be killed by wild dogs. He hated himself enough already.

Dusk twisted round in the window, screeched at him in a fury. She wanted him out of her hair. She needed to concentrate. Sinister things were happening down on the ground. General Rat was up to something.

But, just then, Jay's cap flickered. Silver on black. Dusk's eyes shot to it, She'd meant to have nothing more to do with Boy. Not let him weaken her any further. But she just couldn't help herself.

107

'Present?' she asked, pointing, like a little kid looking in a toy shop window.

'What?' said Jay, thrown for a second. Then he frowned. 'You want my cap?' He liked this cap. He didn't really want to give it to her. But he thought, *Ma'll get me another one.*

He took it off, gently, minding his sore head. Stepped towards her, holding it out. Dusk made a lunge, snatched it, sat it on top of her head.

Jay said, 'No, you don't wear it like that. Look, pull it down low.'

He mimed the actions, 'Like this.'

Dusk pulled it down low, over her long, white-blonde hair.

She watched him intently, her eyes following every detail of his face, his movements. And suddenly she made a picture in her head. Of Curtis, showing her how to comb her hair, put in the hair slide. As she remembered it, her hand slid up to stroke the hair slide. But it was hidden under the cap.

Jay looked like Curtis. Dusk could see Curtis in his face, his gestures. Jay would have been horrified, if he'd known that. The last thing he wanted to do was be like his father.

'Put the peak round the front,' said Jay, 'so it shades your eyes.'

He was very fussy about the finer points of cap wearing. Get it wrong and you could look stupid, even in a really cool cap like his.

'Some kids wear their caps back to front or sideways,'

Jay explained, forgetting how freaky she'd seemed to him, just minutes before. 'But I think that's cheesy.'

He forgot as well she didn't like to be touched. Jay reached out, twitched the cap round on her head. She let him.

There was a desperate struggle going on in Dusk's mind. She shared her life with hawks, not people. People were enemies. She should hate Boy. But her human heart was telling her something different.

Jay looked, critically, at the way Dusk was wearing his cap. He almost added, 'You keep your ears outside. Don't squash 'em under the cap that way.' Boys never did unless they wanted to look like nerds. But he couldn't mime the actions. *And anyway*, he thought, *maybe girls wear caps different.*

Finally, he nodded with approval. Then he said, with echoes of Curtis in his voice, 'Hey, you look good in that. Real cool.'

Dusk pictured the rats swarming over him. It was the kind of death she had nightmares about. Better a clean bite from one of the dogs. It was no good. She couldn't watch him die like that. Dusk sighed. For her, staying alive in Prospect was tough enough already. Keeping Jay alive too was going to complicate things.

Not clever, Dusk told herself, shaking her head at her own stupidity.

Jay said, 'What's the matter. Don't you like the cap?'

'Boy!' said Dusk. 'Come here.' She was pointing out of the window.

Jay stood beside her and looked down on Prospect.

He couldn't see the tangle of luminous trails, like she could. All he could see was a shadowy mass moving along Main Street. It seemed to be alive. Something silver glittered at the head of it.

'What is it?' asked Jay, the hairs already prickling on the back of his neck.

'General Rat's army,' said Dusk.

And Jay could see now, the heaving rodent bodies, hundreds of them. He shuddered. 'Rats,' he murmured. He thought he'd heard some, back there in the store. But he'd never guessed there were that many.

'Gross!' he said to Dusk. 'I seen 'em running over garbage sacks in the city. But they're not dangerous, are they? I mean to people?'

Dusk threw him a look that said, *Are you serious?*

'If the General says "Kill", they kill,' she told Jay, keeping it as simple as she could.

'But not *people*,' insisted Jay.

'Why not people?' asked Dusk, amazed at his ignorance. She laughed out loud – it was the most human sound Jay had heard her make. It really tickled her sense of humour that Jay thought people were special. That the General would say, 'Oh, you're people. Please go free!'

'You telling me I shouldn't go out there? That those rats are dangerous?'

Dusk nodded. 'They *will* kill people,' she told him, to make quite sure he understood.

'Then how come they haven't killed you?' asked Jay. 'You're people.'

Dusk looked at him as if he was crazy, comparing her to

people. People didn't have her powers, they couldn't fly.

'I am Dusk,' she said, as if that explained everything.

Jay slumped down on the floor despairing, his head in his hands. He'd been all psyched up to make a great escape from Prospect, taking her with him. But he didn't know what to do now.

He thought, *Maybe she's lying about the rats*. Maybe, if he went out there, he could say 'Boo!' and they'd all scamper off.

But he couldn't bring himself to risk it. She was wild and weird and scary. But there was something else about her – a kind of authority, even though she only looked about his age – as if she knew what she was talking about.

'So when can I go home?' he asked Dusk.

'Daytime,' said Dusk. She thought she'd mostly forgotten human speech. But she was remembering more words. How to string them together. 'Daytime. When General Rat goes to bed.' She didn't tell him the dogs would be out then. Dusk operated mostly on instinct, in the here and now. Morning was a very long way away.

Jay tried to calm himself down, make himself accept the situation. *It's only a few hours*, he thought, *then I'm out of here*.

Outside, the sky was deep indigo, sprinkled with stars. An owl hooted somewhere.

Jay hadn't realized how tired he was. He was shattered, weary right through to his bones. He was hungry. His leg hurt. 'What kind of place is this?' Jay said, more to himself than to Dusk. 'It's like I'm in a nightmare.'

Dusk, squatting in the window, heard him. But she

111

didn't answer. She didn't have the words to explain life in Prospect. And even if she did, how could Jay understand?

It might look like nature red in tooth and claw. But there were checks and balances, so she and the other predators could coexist. It was a risky, knife-edge existence. But she'd learned to predict their movements, stay alive. Even form alliances with some of them. It was always dangerous in Prospect. But there was a pattern to things, a kind of order. Dusk knew where she fitted in. She had pictures in her head of the way it worked. Day was Wolf's time. Night belonged to the rats. And she was Dusk. She'd earned her place as one of the top predators. She was human enough to feel proud of that.

And human enough to want the boy to know who he was dealing with.

'I am Dusk,' she told him again, without turning round.

Jay forced his eyes open; he'd almost been nodding off. 'That your name?' he asked her. It sounded like she thought she was a queen or something! He felt resentful. How could she have that kind of confidence? Especially a freak like her. When his own self confidence was so shaky.

'That your name? Dusk?' he asked her again.

At last Dusk turned round. She gave him a glare from those mad orange eyes. 'Yes,' she said, as if he'd dared to challenge it.

Jay heard himself boasting, 'I probably saved your life back there. That's a long way to fall, from that window.'

He almost hated himself for saying it. But he just couldn't help it. He wanted her to think, *What a hero!*

Ever since Little Shane, he'd been looking for ways to get his pride back. At school the fight was still hot news. Every day someone had twisted the knife, said something that made him squirm. At times he felt it would follow him all his life, like a curse. That they'd never stop giving him a hard time about it. When he was a wrinkly old man, someone would still be saying, 'Remember when you tried to pick on Little Shane? Thought he was a push-over! You made a big mistake there. He really kicked your ass!' But this girl knew nothing about what happened. It was like making a fresh start.

But she didn't seem impressed. She didn't even seem to understand him. She was still glaring at him, scornfully this time.

Fall? Dusk was thinking. *This boy is stupid!* Didn't he know she could fly?

Instinctively, while she was still looking at him, her hand shot out of the steeple window and snatched a big white moth out the night air. She crammed it into her mouth, its wings still fluttering.

Jay thought, revolted, *For heaven's sake! Why do I care what she thinks? She's an alien!*

He was hungry too. But he didn't dare say, 'You got anything to eat?' She'd probably shove a moth down his throat. His stomach turned, just thinking about it.

He seached in his pocket. There was half a chocolate bar he'd forgotten about. Jay munched it, miserably.

Dusk slid down from the windowsill, squatted in the corner. Her eyes lost that fierce orange glitter. Her third eyelids slid over them, so they looked like smoky suns. She hugged her knees, let her head droop on them and fell asleep instantly, like a baby.

It wasn't like Dusk to let her guard down. Especially with people. She felt superior to them. But she was scared of them too – knew their capacity to inflict harm. Yet she felt safe to fall asleep with Jay. She didn't think he'd hurt her. Otherwise she would have stayed up all night, watching him like a hawk.

Jay watched her, curled up, sleeping. He was more curious now than scared. His mind raced with questions. *Who is she?* he asked himself. *What is she? What's she doing here?*

Dusk twitched like a dog in her sleep. What was she dreaming about?

Jay couldn't keep up the questions. Especially when there were no answers. He felt his own eyelids drooping.

He thought, *I should stay awake.* He shifted to make his bad leg more comfortable, heard the matches in his pocket rattle. He'd forgotten about them. He wished he had a cigarette. For a crazy second, he wondered about playing the pain game, to keep himself alert. Then he thought, *Don't be stupid. What do you want to do that for?* He was in enough pain already.

Images slid through his mind: getting hammered by Little Shane, the crucified hawk, that white dog bursting through the window . . .

Then, just as he was dozing off, something *really* crazy drifted into his head. Jay thought, *What if I took Dusk home to meet Ma? Said, 'Here's my new girlfriend.'* Ma was probably the one person in the world who wouldn't be freaked out. She'd take one look at that T-shirt and say, 'An angel.' Ma had always believed in angels. She'd say, 'Come right in!' Probably bake her some angel cake.

And he'd have to say, 'Ma, she's no angel, she eats rats.'

The thought brought a dreamy grin to his face. Then he moaned, 'My head hurts. My leg hurts. They're gonna keep me awake all night.'

Soon, the only sound in the ivy-covered tower was the gentle breathing of two sleeping people.

11

Curtis woke up. He'd fallen asleep in the cane chair on his front porch. He felt rough. His head was muzzy. His mouth felt full of sand. He was shambling inside to bed, to sleep until he could face the day. But there was something nagging in his mind. Something he should be doing.

Then he remembered. He stumbled into Jay's bedroom. It was empty. *Where's that boy got to?* thought Curtis. He was worried now. Red-blooded teenage boys roamed, he knew that. They sometimes stayed out all night. But what was there to stay out for, up here in the woods?

He ducked his head under the cold water tap, splashed it over his face, gargled with it. *I oughta go out looking for him*, he told himself. Curtis found the keys to the four-by-four in the coffee jar, where he'd dropped them. Went out on to the porch. Then he saw the dog.

It didn't belong to him. Didn't belong to anyone. It was a stray, a sort of rent-a-dog. Men took it out hunting with them sometimes, because it was good at following a scent.

'You hungry, boy?' asked Curtis. The dog whined. Curtis sighed. He'd always had a soft spot for this dog. You thought, *I haven't seen it for months.* You were sure it had died. But you went out one morning and there it was.

'Like a bad penny,' said Curtis, scratching its scrawny neck, under its collar.

He didn't have time to give it anything fancy. He whacked a few hamburgers into the microwave, defrosted them. The dog wolfed them down,

It was when he was giving the dog the hamburgers that Curtis really looked at the collar. 'Who gave you that, boy?' He peered at the plaited leather thong, the metal beads shaped like dice. He'd seen something like it before. Then he remembered. It was round his son's neck.

He thought, *Why should it be Jay's? Could be anybody's.* Lots of kids probably wore stuff like that.

But he had a bad feeling about this. He thought, *I should have looked for him last night.*

He undid the collar, felt the dice cold against his palm. The dog sniffed it, excitedly. Jay had worn the plaited leather thong round his neck for six months, hardly ever taken it off. It had soaked up his sweat.

The dog shot off.

'Damn,' said Curtis, left with the collar dangling from his hand.

He could never follow the dog on foot. He climbed into his battered old four-by-four, scrunched it into gear and drove off in the same direction as the dog.

In the steeple, the first pale ribbons of daylight came fluttering in. They fell on to Jay's sleeping face. But it wasn't that that woke him. It was a great screech of alarm from Dusk.

117

Jay forced open his gummy eyes. Dusk was sitting in the window, with the baseball cap on, gazing down on Prospect. He forced his stiff, aching body into action.

'What's the matter?' He dragged himself over to the window.

Dusk looked agitated, her whole body tense and restless.

'General Rat!' she said, pointing. 'He is out. With his army. In daytime!'

It was totally out of order. Daytime belonged to the dogs. The fragile balance that existed between her, the rats and Wolf was being blown to pieces. Was the General trying to take over the daytime, as well as the night?

It was because of the boy, she was sure. General Rat must have smelled him. Knew he was hiding in Prospect somewhere. Now he was sending out scouts to find him. A human was big, important prey. The General didn't want the dogs to find him first.

Dusk shrieked in fury. 'Go away!' she said to Jay. She forgot about his present; that she'd decided to protect him. She should have known better. People didn't belong in Prospect – they only brought trouble.

'Go away, Boy!' she told him.

She shrieked again, harsh distress calls. They drove the sparrowhawk from her nest. The male soared after her. Dusk called after them, trying to make them come back. But they were already just dots in the blue. Then even her eyes lost sight of them.

Dusk felt totally out of control, as if her world was falling apart.

Jay dragged a hand over his blood-streaked forehead. He was still groggy with sleep. He didn't know what was going on, why Dusk was mad at him again.

He looked out the window. This time he could see Prospect clearly, not in hazy half-light. What he saw snapped his eyes open, startled him awake.

Down in Main Street, the rising sun caught the General's skull plate. It flashed crimson. His bodyguards flanked him. Behind him, his entire army was assembling. They spilled out of the shop. They raced up from their burrows in the ground.

'There are thousands of them,' Jay said.

He could see instantly that the one at the front, the big white one, was in command. His army was a squirming mob, jostling, twisting tails round each other. But they stayed behind him, as if waiting for a signal.

'Dusk, tell me what's happening,' begged Jay.

Dusk heard him talking but it was like a background buzz. She was concentrating on what was happening down on the ground.

Even her ultraviolet vision didn't give her an edge in daylight. She could see some rat signs. But they didn't glow bright and golden like they did when it got dark. She suspected that the General had sent out scouts. But which direction did they go in? Were they heading this way, for the steeple? Usually she could see every urine splash, every greasy smear they left behind.

The rat army was getting frustrated. Some were ripping out each other's fur with their scalpel-sharp teeth. But still the General didn't make his move.

Why is General Rat waiting? thought Dusk. It must be for his scouts to report back.

The General seemed calm and still. But behind him his vicious army was almost boiling over with bloodlust. They had enough brains to know that if the General had brought them out in daylight, something big was about to happen.

Dusk knew they would have to kill soon – or even the General wouldn't be able to control them.

'Go away!' Dusk told Jay again. It was all his fault this had happened. That Prospect had been thrown into chaos. She should have killed him when she had the chance.

'What are you mad at me for?' asked Jay, bewildered. 'I mean, make up your mind. Last night you said, "Stay here"!'

Dusk didn't answer, just glared at him.

'I'm going anyhow,' he told her.

He stared out the window, trying to assess the risks. The rat army was down at the end of Main Street. They didn't seem to be moving. Maybe he could make it to the tree bridge, get back over the fence. His bad leg didn't bother him so much now.

He had one last try, although in his heart he knew it was hopeless. 'You coming with me?'

Dusk hissed defiance. The thought of leaving Prospect filled her with terror. It was where she belonged.

'We could make it,' Jay reassured her, 'if we run.'

She spat in his face.

'What you do that for?' said Jay, disgusted. 'I was only trying to help!' He gave up on her. *She's not worth it*, he thought.

'Your funeral,' he told her, over his shoulder.

He was halfway down the stairs when a dog howled.

Dusk thought, *Wolf is awake.*

The General had heard it too. He stood on his hind legs, sniffed the air.

Jay came back upstairs. He told Dusk, 'Those dogs are out there. No *way* am I going down now.'

Dusk screeched in fury. She felt unsafe, threatened from all sides. To her, it was like riots on the city streets. Law and order in Prospect had broken down.

Wolf had already seen the rat army. Usually in daytime, he was king. He would lead his family right down the middle of Main Street. Like Dusk, he was taken by surprise. Snarling softly, he backed inside the bank again. He took his family out through a hole in the wall. All seven of them slipped into the wilderness.

Dusk saw them. She thought, *Where is Wolf going?* Her hawk eyes tracked them, saw every move they made. She shuffled further out on the ledge so she could see them better.

Jay thought, *Oh no, she's not trying that again!*

But Dusk didn't throw herself off. She would fly later if all hope failed.

Jay sighed with relief. Dusk was his link with the outside, checking the ground, trying to interpret the signs. He didn't want to be trapped up here alone. He thought of himself squatting on the stinking floor among the fur and blood and feathers, not knowing when it was safe to go down.

There'd be nothing to do but think. Play the pain game

until his matches ran out. All his monsters, so red in tooth and claw since the fight with Little Shane, would come to torment him. He thought, *I'd go crazy.*

But with Dusk here, it couldn't happen. You couldn't hide in yourself, make yourself suicidal, when she was around. That life force she had wouldn't let you. It was so vivid, like a wild creature's, so fierce and brightly burning. You couldn't help but pay attention. Those demons inside you got forgotten. They fled back into darkness.

I'm glad she's with me, Jay thought.

The General's troops were like caged tigers, just waiting to be let loose. Dusk was trying to watch them and, at the same time, track Wolf and his family through the wilderness. She tried to shade her eyes with her hands. They worked best in gentle half-light. Her third eyelids slid over. But it wasn't enough to stop the sun dazzling her. She screeched in frustration.

'Pull your cap down,' said Jay.

Dusk had forgotten she'd got it on. She yanked it down, so the long peak bathed her light-sensitive eyes in shadow, cut out the sun's glare. She could see everything that was going on.

'Good,' she told Jay.

'It's a good cap,' agreed Jay, nodding.

All at once Dusk's rage against him evaporated. She was suddenly glad that he hadn't left the steeple. Prospect was in meltdown around her. Her hawks had deserted her, General Rat was out in daylight, and she had no idea how Wolf was going to react. In all the confusion, at least Boy seemed to be on her side. She didn't even mind that he

122

was human. Humans were the least of her worries now.

'When I get out of here,' Jay told her, 'I'm going to get another cap just like it.'

Dusk's eyes spotted something. They zoomed in, like a camera lens.

'Dog,' she said.

'Where?' said Jay, springing forwards, his heart beating wildly.

Dusk pointed, way out into the scrubland, near the fence. She could see the same red tick, like a tiny blood balloon, nestling in the dog's ear.

'Where?' said Jay. He thought she'd meant Wolf and his family. He saw the long grass rippling, then his hound dog came out into the open. It was heading straight as an arrow for the steeple. It looked excited, its ferny tail wagging, its tongue lolling out. It had only just made it through the storm drain. The pipe had collapsed behind it. The dog didn't know it, but there was no way back for him.

Jay screeched at it from the tower, 'Go back! Go back!'

But the dog couldn't hear him. Jay was frantic. 'Dumb dog!' he yelled at it. 'Go back!' Didn't it remember what happened yesterday? But the dog was on autopilot, too busy following its nose to think about danger.

'Dumb dog,' whispered Jay to himself, hopelessly.

'Wolf is coming,' Dusk told him.

Jay didn't even think about it. He acted purely on instinct. He clattered down the stairs, pushed open the armoured door. If the dog wouldn't go back, he was going to have to fetch it into the steeple, with him and Dusk.

123

He could hear Dusk behind him crying out, 'Boy! Stay here!' But he didn't stop.

Jay went racing out the church doors into brilliant sunlight. He skidded to a stop, screwed up his eyes, couldn't see anything except glare.

Then, '*Yip, yip, yip yip.*' He heard an hysterical high-pitched barking.

His head whipped round. It was the hound dog on the edge of the scrubland, out in the open. It didn't have a chance.

A snarling white fury came streaking out of the long grass. It was Wolf's mate. She grabbed the dog by the back of the neck, shook it once, like a rag. Then loped off, back into the tall grass, with the limp body dangling from her jaws.

They've just killed my dog, thought Jay.

The shock was so great that his mind, his body, seemed to switch off. He should have run back into the steeple. But he just stood there, helpless, frozen to the spot.

From the steeple, Dusk recognized what was wrong with him. She saw that paralysed reaction in her prey all the time.

Wolf, with his sons behind him, trotted out into the open. They lay down and watched Jay quietly, eyes bright, tongues lolling out. The only sound was their eager panting. They were waiting for him to run.

What had happened to the hound dog was slowly penetrating Jay's brain. His whole body started to shake. But he still didn't move from the spot.

Dusk could see Jay needed help. This time there was no

struggle in her mind. She put her hands up to her new cap, checked it was secure on her head. Then threw herself out the window.

Jay watched her open-mouthed. But she didn't fall to the ground, broken and bloody. She crashed into the ivy, clung there like a monkey. She was going to need a weapon. Dusk pulled her pitchfork out of the ivy. It fitted into her hand like an old friend. She knew every groove she'd worn in the wood. She came clambering down.

Dusk lived every day on her hawk instincts, but also her human wit. As she padded softly towards Jay and the dogs, careful to make no sudden moves, her brain was racing. She was going to try and bargain with Wolf for Jay's life.

At the other end of Prospect, the General didn't know that his prey had broken cover. He wasn't even sure yet where Jay was holed up. No scouts had found him. But he started moving his army. They'd waited too long in the hot sun.

He moved them slowly, conducting a full-scale search, sending troops into every building to flush out the human. Some troops rebelled, tried to push past him. But his body-guards forced them back, savaging those who didn't obey.

No more rats broke rank.

The General was pleased. Only he could have turned this rabble of rat psychopaths into a disciplined fighting force. This was an important test for them – their first taste of human prey. And it was a big day for the General himself. It meant he was one step nearer to taking over the world.

12

Dusk strolled towards Jay. She held her head high, she didn't hurry. There was even a slight smile on her face, as if she was enjoying herself, as if this was all a game.

Her pitchfork was balanced very lightly in her hand, like she was carrying it accidentally and didn't mean to use it.

Show no fear, her brain told her. Not even any tension. It was one of the most important rules when dealing with Wolf and his family. Wolf wasn't cunning like the General. He didn't plan. He obeyed much more primitive instincts. Dusk, part hawk, part human, could understand them both.

Wolf watched her calmly with his yellow eyes.

Jay, still dazed by the horror of the hound dog's death, desperately tried to kick-start his brain. Wolf's mate was sneaking closer, wriggling on her belly through the grass.

Jay almost shouted a warning: 'Watch the white dog!' But Dusk seemed so confident, so in control of the situation, that Jay kept quiet.

She's smiling! thought Jay amazed. As if there weren't seven hungry dogs watching her every move.

He started to walk towards her on shaky legs.

'Boy,' said Dusk. 'Stay still.'

Wolf's family weren't predictable. There was one son, the one with the white muzzle. He was the biggest and strongest of the brothers. He was looking to take over Wolf's place as pack leader.

It was him she was watching, out of the corner of her eye. He was circling out into the scrubland, to cut off their escape route back to the steeple. But Dusk could see him. She could see the metallic blue flash of the flies buzzing over his head.

Dusk looked casual, unconcerned, as if she was taking a Sunday stroll in the park. But she was one hundred per cent alert to the present moment. Fully alive. Every nerve responsive to what was happening around her, to the subtlest shifts in the balance of power. Ready to snatch any opportunity.

Jay tried to copy her cool. His nerves shrieked at him, *Run!* But he forced himself to stay in control. Blocked that image of Wolf's mate with his dog dangling from her jaws out of his mind.

He even tried to hold his head high, face the dogs with Dusk's look of haughty indifference. Although without his cap to hide under, the hot sun felt like it was boiling his brain.

Dusk was wondering what her next move would be. Then one of the General's scouts came snuffling out of the grass.

She moved so fast Jay couldn't follow it. Her throwing net whisked through the air. Then she was above her prey, stabbing down with the pitchfork again and again. You couldn't take any chances with rats.

'Jesus!' said Jay, who'd never seen her hunt before.

Dusk flashed a furious glance at him. It meant, 'Boy, shut up.'

With the dead rat swinging from her hand by the tail, she walked, very slowly, up to Wolf. His mate growled. But all the time Dusk had her eye on his son, creeping up behind her.

She laid the rat down as a gift, in front of Wolf. Then backed off.

For a moment, it seemed to be working. Jay thought, *He's going to let us go*. There was a long silence. All you could hear was the frantic buzz of trapped flies from a patch of tall, straggly pitcher plants.

Then Wolf's son came bursting out of the pitcher plants, barking. Jay almost jumped out of his skin. Wolf's son was slavering, out of control. His white fangs dripped froth.

'Run,' said Dusk. 'Fast.'

She dumped her pitchfork as she ran to give herself more speed. It was no use anyway, against a mad dog.

Jay went after her. His brain was a blur. But Dusk's was still working, thinking tactics. She steered clear of Main Street, where the General was beginning to wonder why his scout hadn't come back. She raced round the back of the houses. This was no time for quiet sneaking. She crashed through the wilderness. A tree root tripped her up. Dusk leaped to her feet, still running. She was heading for the lily pond, the one place in Prospect that both dogs and rats avoided.

Dusk stopped running. Panting hard, she hung on to a tree by the pond. She didn't think Jay would keep up, not with his injured leg. But he wasn't far behind.

When he'd stopped struggling for breath, seeing red swirls in front of his eyes, Jay straightened up. 'Have to give up smoking,' he gasped. Dusk was watching him curiously, as if he was some kind of strange specimen.

'What do we do now?' he asked her.

'Stay here,' said Dusk.

She was waiting to see what Wolf would do. She didn't think he would follow them. Especially not here. She was right about both those things. Wolf usually avoided the lily pond. And he wasn't interested in her and Jay. But he was heading this way all the same. He was tracking his out-of-control son. Wolf had decided it was time for a showdown.

The son, breaking the strict hierarchy of the dog pack, was hunting Dusk and Jay all by himself.

'There's a dog,' Jay shouted a warning. 'Look, there!'

'*Shhhh*,' said Dusk, putting a finger to her lips, just like Curtis did to quieten her at SERU.

'Get down!' Jay hissed.

They flattened themselves into the reeds. Instinctively Dusk's hand shot out. She grabbed a cockroach. Crunch. Even in a crisis, she never missed a chance to eat.

Jay noticed. But this time he didn't even shudder. He just accepted it. She was Dusk. Eating bugs and rats was what she did.

Very cautiously, he parted the reeds. His hands didn't tremble, not much. He was surprised about that. He wasn't going to pieces, like after the fight with . . .

I don't want to hear any of that old shit, Jay told his brain. It was now that mattered. He was in Prospect *now*, with Dusk. Being hunted by wild dogs. But his brain was still dredging up bogeymen from another world . . .

He blocked Little Shane out. Made his mind focus on the moment.

Wolf's son had picked up their scent. He was on the other side of the lily pond, sniffing at the water's edge.

'He's there!' hissed Jay.

Dusk thought, *Why is Boy so noisy?*

Wolf's son couldn't keep quiet either. He should have sneaked up on them. But he wasn't patient like Wolf. He wanted to tell his prey, 'Here I am.' He wanted to chase them and bark a lot. He started barking now.

Wolf came bursting through the trees. His son stopped barking. Turned and faced him.

Dusk watched, her heart fluttering. Would Wolf's son grovel on his belly, give in to his father?

No chance. Wolf's son cocked his leg, as if to scent-mark his territory. Then he bared his teeth and growled. He was challenging his father's authority.

Dusk gripped the grass with tense fingers. The social structure in Prospect was changing so fast she didn't know where she'd stand at the end of it all, where she'd fit in. Except she didn't doubt one thing. She knew, whatever happened, Boy would be with her.

She knew too, that Wolf just couldn't teach his wayward

son a lesson. Give him a few quick nips as if he was still a puppy. Wolf would have to fight him. Even to the death.

'Don't Wolf,' said Dusk. She didn't want Wolf to die. There was a bond between them that went back beyond Prospect. Once upon a time they had both been in cages at SERU. Dusk shuddered at the memory.

Wolf's son was big and strong and two years younger. Wolf was getting slow, too used to lazing around while his family did the hunting. In a one-to-one fight with his son, Dusk wasn't sure Wolf could win.

Jay heard her whisper, 'Run, Wolf.'

He thought, amazed, *She cares about that dog*. Jay should have known she had human emotions. She'd just risked her life to save him. But Jay couldn't deal with that yet. Since Little Shane, he'd got so used to thinking, *You're pathetic*, that it was hard to believe anyone felt different.

He understood her feelings about the dog though. He could really relate to them. Jay had cared about his hound dog that way, even though he'd only just adopted him. He shut his mind to the awful image of the hound dog's death. He couldn't cope with that now either.

Wolf crouched, the hair bristling along his spine. His son sprang. The two dogs collided in mid-air, white teeth snapping. They dropped to the ground, attacked again instantly, in a savage flurry of snarls and bites.

Wolf yelped. His son had got him by the throat. The son held on, shaking Wolf as if he was a rabbit. Wolf was wrestled to the ground. You could see the white fur on his belly.

Now Dusk knew Wolf wouldn't win. His son was

too powerful. Dusk wished she'd kept her pitchfork. She could have evened up the odds.

But Wolf wasn't quite defeated yet. He was struggling to get up, his body thrashing and writhing. The young dog kept his grip. But his legs were scrabbling in the mud. He was slipping down the bank towards the pond. His back paws were already in the water.

Then Wolf's son just vanished.

There was scarcely a splash. Something clamped on to his back legs and dragged him under the lily pads.

It was a very efficient snatch. There was a swirl of water on the surface, some bubbles. In seconds, the surface of the pond was still. Even the white waterlily flowers stopped trembling.

There was an eerie silence. Then Wolf started snarling at the water, his whole body quivering.

Jay said, 'What the hell was that?'

He thought he'd seen a scaly snake head slide out of the lily leaves. But it wasn't a snake, it was warty, like a toad. And it had a cruel parrot's beak.

Jay had never seen anything like it.

The snapping turtle in the lily pond had started out as somebody's pet. They'd kept it in a glass tank. It had been very cute, coin-sized, with a dimpled shell. But it had grown very fast, until it was big enough to rip off a baby's arm. Its beak could shear through bone. Its body was armoured with shell, hard as concrete. Even Dusk's pitchfork couldn't have pierced that.

Its owner had dumped it in the lily pond when Prospect was evacuated. And there it had carried on growing. It caught fish in its snapping jaws and drowned ducks and moorhens, pulling them down by their legs. Once it had nabbed a rat that was swimming across. It had never taken anything as big as a dog before. Most of the time it lurked at the bottom of the pond, disguised as a rock. Invisible, even to Dusk's all-seeing eyes.

Dusk jumped up, backed away from the pond. She wasn't sure what it was. But she knew a top predator when she saw one.

She didn't run though. She was watching Wolf. His business here was finished – why didn't he lope off?

Instead he did something totally unexpected. He growled at her, showing his white fangs. The fighting fit was still on him. His jaws frothed, his red eyes seemed to be swimming in blood. Dusk knew he was very dangerous. Even she couldn't expect mercy.

'Run!' said Jay. 'It's our only chance.'

Dusk knew it was no chance at all. She heard herself scream in fear and fury. There was anarchy in Prospect. Dusk knew the situation was desperate.

If she'd been alone, in the steeple, she would have said, 'Dusk, fly!' with a smile on her face. She'd have spread her arms. Trusted herself to the wind and warm air currents.

But she had Boy to think about now.

Suddenly she plonked herself down in the grass, arms hugging her knees tightly. Jay thought, *What's going on?*

Dusk had amazed him more than once since he'd met her. Now she did something that seemed lunatic. She put a finger to her lips. 'SSHHHH!' she said. 'Boy, sit down.'

He was just about to shriek at her, demented, 'For God's sake, what are you *doing*?'

But the words died in his throat. Her orange eyes were gazing straight into his own. He felt hypnotized by their power and brilliance, like a rabbit caught in car headlights.

Wolf was way beyond being bribed by gifts of dead rats. He was out of control – on the very edge of attacking them.

He circled them growling. Saliva dripped from his jaws on to the grass stems. Every so often his body shuddered. He made a rush at them, barking. Jay flinched. But this time, Wolf didn't bite. He backed off to make another run.

'Boy, sit down,' said Dusk. 'Slow,' she added.

'Jay, my name's Jay,' he said. It seemed a crazy thing to say in a crisis. 'Jay,' he insisted again.

So Dusk used his name, kept her voice strong and steady. 'Jay, sit down.'

She didn't once look at Wolf, as if he wasn't important.

Jay's heart was hammering. His brain was a shrieking chaos. But with a superhuman effort, he copied Dusk. Sat down cross-legged facing her, as if they were having a pow-wow. Tried to make his limbs stop shaking, his brain still. Then Jay felt his eyes slide to the right. He couldn't help it; he had to see what Wolf was doing.

'Don't look at dog,' said Dusk. 'Look at me.'

Jay focused again on her eyes. Felt himself grow calmer, as if there was powerful magic at work.

That muscle was twitching again in his cheek, like

a heartbeat. He couldn't do anything about that. Let it twitch.

Wolf snarled. Was he making another rush?

Dusk saw Jay's eyes wandering. 'Talk,' she said to him.

What about? thought Jay. She seemed almost relaxed, as if they were sitting in the school yard at breaktime, having a chat. But crazy as her behaviour seemed, Jay understood it.

Act normal, he told himself, *like the dog doesn't exist.*

Jay searched his brain. What do boys and girls talk about? He couldn't remember. He could be with girls a whole hour and not say one word. Jay wasn't good at making small talk – not with girls anyway.

Wolf was sniffing at his back. Jay could feel the dog's hot breath through his T-shirt. The muscle in his cheek went manic. He was maybe two seconds away from having his throat torn out.

'Don't look at dog,' hissed Dusk urgently 'Talk to me.'

Jay tried to block out the dog, connect only with Dusk's orange eyes.

'I don't know what to talk about,' Jay started. He was going to talk to her about his life before Prospect. About school, his friends, Dad being a drunk, the grief he caused Ma because he didn't believe. His fight with Little Shane and how it had wrecked his life, still haunted him. How he'd walked home afterwards alone, crying, smashing his fists into walls.

But, suddenly, he didn't want to repeat all that heart-ache. He was sick of it. Something else to talk about opened up in his mind like a brilliant flower.

And he knew, at this moment, what he believed. His words tumbled out, intense, excited.

'It's *now* that matters,' he told Dusk. 'So why do they keep telling us it isn't? Like Ma says, "You'll get your reward in heaven. Just wait." And Curtis says, "I'll be a better Dad – some day. Just wait." Well, I can't wait. All that's just crap, trying to stop you living.'

Jay stopped. He hardly knew what he was saying, or if it made sense. The words came gushing up from somewhere deep inside him.

'It's now that matters,' he insisted. And when he heard himself say it again so passionately, he felt an amazing freedom, a new start. All the burdens of the past just fell away. It was so simple. Why hadn't he seen it before? 'Now,' he said again. 'Just you and me.'

Grrrrr!

Dusk's head swivelled round. Jay followed her gaze – he couldn't help it. She was looking straight at Wolf. She'd said not to do that! But Wolf wasn't there. He was on the other side of the lily pond, his nose buried in grass, sniffing deeply like any dog out for a walk.

He'd come back to his senses. He peed a few times over the scent marks his dead son had made, just to show he was still the boss.

Then he loped off into the high grass.

'Good,' Dusk nodded at Jay. 'Wolf gone.'

Dusk didn't know how it worked. But sometimes, if she could cut a threat out of her consciousness, act unconcerned, as if it didn't exist, then the threat got the message: 'You are nothing.' And disappeared.

136

Suddenly Jay started trembling. 'You're not even scared,' he said to Dusk. 'How do you do that?'

Dusk frowned at him. That frown said, 'Are you serious?' She unlocked her arms from around her knees. Her knees were shaking, just like his, uncontrollably. She let him watch for a few seconds to make sure he understood. Then grabbed her knees with both hands, crunched them violently together, made them stop.

'You *are* afraid,' whispered Jay. He shot her a quick, sympathetic grin. 'I'm glad about that,' he said, 'cos I'm terrified.'

Dusk sprang up. Pulled down her cap. Together they plunged back into the wilderness.

13

Curtis had lost the dog. He was driving round the back roads aimlessly, looking for Jay.

He braked, his tyres skidding on gravel, poked his head out the window.

'Hey, Mrs Olafsen, you seen a boy pass this way? Maybe with a dog?'

He forced himself to be pleasant. He couldn't stand Mrs Olafsen. And it wasn't because she used live pigeons as bait to poison hawks. That didn't bother him much. It was just the country way. And anyhow, he'd seen scientists at SERU do much crueller things to animals. Only they did it secretly, behind closed doors.

Mrs Olafsen gave him a cheery wave. Her blue eyes twinkled at him. 'Curtis! Haven't seen you round here for a long time. Yes, I seen a boy. It was yesterday though, early morning. I seen him take off, chasing his dog.' She pointed through the trees. 'He went that way.'

Curtis stared. There was nothing that way, through the trees. Except Prospect.

I didn't take him seriously, thought Curtis. Maybe he did find a way over that electrified fence. He started to drive. He was truly worried now. *That dumb kid. His Ma's going to kill me if anything's happened to him.*

Dusk and Jay were trying to reach the church. They'd come out of the scrubland. They'd almost made it, when the General and his bodyguards came bounding round the corner of the church. The General saw them both, caught out in the open. And knew all his patience had been rewarded.

His vast rat army came streaming up behind him. They were squeaking in excitement, jostling, pushing. But he wouldn't have to hold them much longer. He stood on his hind legs, ready to give the signal.

Wolf was out in the wilderness somewhere, licking his wounds. He'd taken the dog pack, only six of them now, to a safe distance. He knew there was no way they could take on the rats.

Jay stared at the rat army in horror. He couldn't see the end of them. They seemed to stretch away forever. Just a writhing swarm of naked tails, fur, teeth and bright, blood-hungry eyes.

He thought, *We'll never make it to the steeple.* The General had already sent an advance party swarming into the church, to cut them off.

Could they make it to the fence? He could see the tree bridge, the only way out of Prospect. But there was scrubland to cross, with only straggly pitcher plants for cover. That's where the rats would catch them.

'There's a way out,' Jay told Dusk. 'I know how to get over the fence.'

'No!' Dusk shook her head. The thought of leaving Prospect, even with Jay, threw her into panic. She looked round wildly for some other escape route. She knew the rats meant to eat them alive.

'Come on,' begged Jay. 'I'm not going without you.'

But the ground was alive. A rippling grey sea was rushing towards them. The General had let his army loose.

Jay swallowed hard, mechanically wiped the sweat off his hands on the side of his shorts. Something rattled in his pocket. Matches.

He scrabbled for them. Opened the box the wrong way up. Matches flew everywhere, were lost in the grass.

There was only one match left. He struck it. The tiny flame flickered. He cupped his hand round it to protect it. The rats' eager squeaking rose like an evil cloud over their heads.

Jay crouched down. Set fire to the base of a tall, dried-up pitcher plant. It flared up, *whoosh*, like a torch. The flames started spreading through the parched bushes. Suddenly the scrubland was blooming with fiery orange flowers.

Dusk shrieked. She hated fire. She threw yearning glances back at her steeple. But the rats and the fire were between her and her home. Dusk knew it was a lost hope. She ran for the fence with Jay.

Behind them the flames had become a fire monster. As they ran they could hear it crackling, feel its heat.

Dusk shrieked distress calls. She couldn't even see her steeple any more.

Jay glanced over his shoulder. Where were the rat hordes? A grey smoky haze was drifting across the scrubland. Were they still coming?

'You've got to climb up there,' Jay told Dusk, pointing to where the two trees met. 'Then you can get across.'

A hot wind was scorching their faces. Through the smoke they could see fuzzy yellow fireballs. They were blazing trees.

Dusk scrambled up through the branches. Jay followed clumsily, dragging his bad leg. After all that running it seemed to be going numb on him.

He was heaving himself up through the branches when something came hurtling through the wall of smoke and flames. It sizzled on the electric fence and dropped down. It was a rat.

Another flew past them like a kamikaze pilot and got fried on the wire. Another came and another. The General had sent them on a suicide mission.

Dusk was clinging to the topmost branches. Sparks from the fire smouldered on her clothes.

'Go across!' urged Jay.

A fresh assault of rats came, crashed into the electric wire. The fence sparked, shuddered.

'Dusk!' pleaded Jay, as the shockwaves made the interlocked trees vibrate. 'I'm coming right behind you. I promise.'

The General had found the steeple door open. He and his bodyguards had swarmed up the steps. From up there he had a bird's eye view. He had seen his prey escaping. But he had seen the fence rock too. And suddenly he changed his plans. Taking over from humans, becoming top species, was closer than he thought.

Dusk wriggled like a lizard over the bridge of branches. Jay lost sight of her in the tangled branches.

Jay hauled himself on his belly after her. He was coughing now, his eyes watery and smarting from smoke. Just beneath him, he could see the fence hanging with bodies. Every time a new wave of rats hit it, it shook, sent out blue sparks. Gave off a sizzling sound like bacon frying.

Jay hung on as the bridge swayed wildly. His bad leg slipped over the edge, dangled uselessly. The tip of his trainer almost brushed the fence.

Dusk looked back. Jay wasn't behind her. He'd deserted her too. Why had she trusted a human? Panic and despair almost overwhelmed her. But there was still one hope left . . .

His face twisted with effort, Jay pulled his leg back up, crawled into the oak.

He thought Dusk would be safe by now, would have slithered to the ground. Then with a heart-wrenching shock, he saw her, still crouched in the top branches. She was flapping her arms desperately. She was trying to fly. A blissful smile slid over her face. She had absolute faith. It had been her dream for so long.

'No, Dusk!' Jay reached out tried to grab her. 'People can't fly.'

It was too late. Dusk didn't even know he was there. She was in a world of her own. Somewhere he couldn't reach her.

Dusk hurled herself from the top of the mighty oak. She was flying. The wind caressing her body. The warm thermals cradling her, lifting her up . . .

Then, with a shriek, she plummeted. And knew, in one frantic second, that there was no escape. That she couldn't fly, after all.

She came hurtling down from the sky like a stone – straight into Curtis's arms.

At the same moment there was a crunching sound of metal bending and twisting. The fence's electric current shorted in a firework display of sparks. Jay, in the oak's lower branches, heard the trees groan and crack like gunshot. Felt them toppling. He jumped.

Rats were still hurling themselves at the fence as a whole section, ten metres long, collapsed and took the two trees with it.

Dusk started fighting immediately, to get out of the grip of whoever had caught her.

'Dusk!' At first Curtis was too stunned to defend himself. 'I thought you were dead.' He tried to hold her tighter. She screeched, terrible high-pitched distress calls. Raked at his eyes with her nails, spat at him. A smoke haze drifted all around them.

'It's me, Dusk. Remember me?' coughed Curtis, trying to hold on to her.

But she was too manic to recognize him. She was a wild fury, trying to bite his neck, like hawks do, severing their victim's spine with one snap.

'Hey!' screamed Curtis, loosening his grip, one hand flying to his bleeding neck.

It was all the chance Dusk needed. She was off, darting through the trees.

Jay staggered up from the grass, where he'd fallen. Saw Dusk streaking off. Thought, *She's still alive!* He couldn't believe it, the distance she'd fallen. *Maybe she flew after all*, he thought.

Then he saw Curtis. 'Dad!' He went running over.

'I just caught her,' said Curtis in a dazed voice. 'But I couldn't keep hold of her.' He'd lost her for the second time. There was blood trickling from his neck, soaking his shirt. But he didn't seem to notice. He was still staring after her.

'Dusk!' he shouted. But Dusk had disappeared.

Jay said, 'We got to catch her. She's gonna get hurt!'

It was only when they were in the four-by-four with Curtis driving, off-roading, crashing through the trees after Dusk, that Jay thought, *How did Dad know her name?*

The other surprising thing was that Curtis had been there, just when he was needed.

'You came looking for me!' said Jay.

'Don't sound so surprised,' said Curtis.

Behind them smoke made the sky black. Lurid against it was a pillar of orange and crimson. It was Dusk's tower going up in flames. The two sparrowhawks had come back. Only when it started falling, a blazing ruin, did they abandon their eggs and swoop off over the woods. This time for good.

The snapping turtle saw the water surface reflect red, then gold, like neon lights, as the fire flashed by overhead. He was safe though, at the bottom of the lily pond.

The General was safe too. He'd left the tower with his faithful bodyguards, just before it caught fire. They'd taken refuge in the damp, moss-lined crevice where Dusk's water supply came bubbling up out of the ground. Now they were crossing the scrubland, a small band of about fifty. The soil was smouldering, the pitcher plants black and crunchy. The fire had swept over the scrubland and moved on. It was raging now in the buildings on Main Street. The rat HQ, with the babies left in the nests, had already been consumed by flames.

The General stopped where the fence had collapsed to survey the damage. It was a terrible scene of carnage. Most of his soldiers were fried to a crisp. Their bodies were piled ten deep on the ground. But he didn't give them a second thought. They'd served their purpose, brought the fence down so the General could move what was left of his army out of Prospect.

Some, besides his bodyguards, were still alive. The ones who had flung themselves at the fence after the current failed. They fell in behind him. All the rats went bounding across the bodies of their comrades. The General knew his prey had escaped. But that hardly mattered now. Soon there would be a much better supply of humans. He was going south to the nearest city. He would lie low for a while, maybe in the sewers, until he had more soldiers. That wouldn't take long – female rats can give birth to seventy babies a year.

Then one night, when the humans were sleeping, he would lead his rat army out on to the streets and into their houses.

Wolf and his family watched the rats go. Then they picked their way through the burned rat bodies, their noses wrinkling in disgust at the smell.

The dogs' fur was singed and sooty. They had survived, just, by outrunning the fire. Wriggling on their bellies under the smoke, leaping through sudden gaps as the flame surged this way, then that.

They stopped to drink from a ditch to cool their throats. The water was slimy with green scum but they gulped it down. Then they set off with Wolf leading. Soon the woods swallowed them up.

Wolf wasn't going south to the city. He was taking his family north to even more remote territory. North, where humans were scarce and real wolves still roamed the forests.

14

'There she is!' said Jay.

Dusk wasn't running. She was crouched in a grassy clearing. Sunlight and shadows flickered all around her, over her. But she stayed dead still.

She didn't even notice the four-by-four creeping up. She'd seen something. Her eyes were fixed on it with that fierce, unblinking stare.

She's alive, Curtis was thinking. That still amazed him. How had she escaped the fire at SERU? How had she survived all this time? It seemed to be some kind of miracle.

Food! Dusk was thinking. Her hawk instincts had kicked in. It was a blessed relief. It stopped the pain for a moment of knowing that she was lost and alone. And that she couldn't fly, like hawks do.

Her orange eyes sparkled with their old brilliance. She grinned, like she used to do back in Prospect. This was easy prey. It was injured. She wouldn't even have to use her throwing net.

What's she after? thought Jay.

The shifting light patterns confused him. But he knew

that look of intense concentration, that hunter's crouch, her body poised, on a hair trigger.

Then he saw it too. Something fluttery. It was on the far side of the clearing. Another flutter. Jay tried to make it out. Curtis sneaked the four-by-four a little closer.

'It's a pigeon,' said Jay. It was struggling to beat its wings, take off. But one wing was drooping, dragging on the grass. And then Jay saw that its feet were tethered to a stake driven into the ground.

The crucified hawk flashed through Jay's mind.

'No, Dusk!' screamed Jay, throwing himself out of the vehicle.

He tripped, picked himself up, carried on running. 'It's poisoned. Leave it! Leave it!' he yelled, like you would to a dog.

Dusk sprang. In one swift movement, she snatched the pigeon, snapped its neck. When Jay reached her, she was already plucking off breast feathers, stuffing the bird into her mouth.

He ripped it off her.

He thought, *Mustn't let her run!* He held her, shrieking, in a bear hug. She lashed out at him with her long dirty nails. He had to twist his face away, or she'd have blinded him.

Curtis came stumbling up. 'Let her go! She don't like being touched.'

But Dusk had suddenly gone limp. She was sagging in his arms.

'She just ate poisoned bait!' Jay told Curtis, his eyes wild and scared.

Curtis looked at the dead pigeon. Saw the tethers on his legs. 'It's that bitch, Mrs Olafsen.'

'We got to get Dusk to hospital, Dad.'

'No,' said Curtis. 'No hospital.' It was a sure way for the military to find her. 'Let me have her.' He knelt down, took Dusk from Jay, stuck a finger down her throat.

Dusk gagged, threw up violently. Curtis struggled to hold her head. He tried to make comforting noises. 'It'll be all right. It'll be all right.' But his arms were shaking.

Jay hated people being sick. The sight of it, the smell. He fought to control his own heaving stomach. 'Think she got rid of it all, Dad? She's throwing her guts up.'

'I don't know,' said Curtis. 'I don't think there's anything else to come up. Just get her in the vehicle.'

'What if she dies, Dad?' said Jay. 'We should take her to hospital.'

'I told you, boy!' barked Curtis. 'No hospital.'

Dusk was still retching and shivering.

Curtis scooped her up. She didn't try to fight him, was way beyond recognizing him as someone who'd once been kind to her. Her head was flopping, her arms dangling. Jay's baseball cap rolled off her head.

As he carried her back to the vehicle, Curtis thought he glimpsed a movement between the trees. But at that moment he had more urgent things on his mind.

Jay trudged after Curtis, feeling helpless, bewildered. Behind them, Dusk's cap lay forgotten in the clearing. A shaft of sunlight caught it. It glittered like a bright star, silver against black.

Jay didn't want to sit in the back with Dusk, see her

suffering. He wished Ma was here. She was good with sick people.

'You sit in the back with her,' he begged Curtis. What if she died on him? Right there, while he watched? She looked half dead already. Sweating, her skin grey. Her brilliant orange eyes, so vivid with life, were dull and unseeing, like the crucified hawk's . . .

'Jesus, let her live,' said Jay. There he was again, praying to someone he didn't believe in. But like Ma said, who else was there to ask?

'Let me drive,' he begged Curtis.

'You remember how?' asked Curtis.

'Course I do!' said Jay, indignantly.

As the four-by-four started up, juddered away, Mrs Olafsen came out from the shadows between the trees. She'd come back to check her hawk trap, collect any dead bodies. She'd been watching for some time.

In the back seat, Curtis was saying, 'Don't go to sleep on me, Dusk. Stay awake.'

Driving again after so long took all Jay's concentration. He gripped the wheel so tight his knuckles were white, like bone. But as he fought with the controls, he felt his eyes stinging. Told himself, through gritted teeth, *Don't start crying*.

'Drive faster,' ordered Curtis from the back seat. 'Her breathing's too slow.'

'Dad!' screamed Jay, almost hysterical. 'We got to take her to a doctor! She's gonna die!'

'She's better off dead,' said Curtis, 'than if the military got her. Just drive.'

Back at Curtis's shack, Dusk wanted to sleep but Curtis said, 'We got to keep her awake until the poison gets out of her system.'

They walked her up and down between them, her feet dragging, her head lolling as if her neck was broken. They shook her, shouted her name. 'Dusk! Stay awake!' Tears streamed, unashamed, down Jay's face. He felt so helpless, so exhausted. But he didn't ask Curtis again to take her to hospital. He didn't know how Curtis knew about Dusk – he hadn't had a chance to ask him. But, for once, he thought, *Dad knows what he's doing.*

Curtis had to clear his junk out of the way to make a space. As they walked Dusk round the room, Jay stopped calling on Jesus to save Dusk. He was tired of begging and begging, like Ma said you had to do. It was humiliating. He thought, *What's he want me to do? Crawl? What am I doing asking him anyhow? He doesn't exist.*

Jay suddenly felt very small and alone.

Then he remembered Dusk at the lily pond. Where she'd willed him to control his fear of Wolf. 'Don't look at dog. Look at me.' He felt better, just hearing her calm voice in his head.

'Talk to me,' she'd said by the lily pond. So he did.

'You're gonna stay alive? Right!' he said, fiercely. 'I'm gonna make sure you do! Are you listening? Don't you dare die on me! I'm not going to let you!' Just saying that made him feel stronger.

'Go it, son,' said Curtis, with a weary grin. 'That's telling her.'

And suddenly Jay realized he wasn't on his own. Dusk's

voice was in his head, even though she couldn't talk to him now. Dad was with him too, plodding up and down with him, wearing a groove in the carpet.

'Hard work, ain't it, son?' said Curtis. Jay gave him a shaky smile over Dusk's wobbling head.

Hours seemed to pass. They dragged her up and down, up and down with Jay telling her she wasn't allowed to die and Curtis trudging, more and more slowly but with a dogged look on his face.

Then at last Curtis said, 'I think we can let her rest now.'

She collapsed on the couch. Curtis went for a blanket, tucked it round her. Dusk's hand suddenly flopped out from under the blanket. It dangled, pitifully. He tucked it back in so she wouldn't get cold.

Jay flung himself down by the couch, his heart racing. 'She's not dead, is she?'

'No,' said Curtis, throwing himself down in a chair. It creaked under his weight. 'She's still alive.'

Jay had forgotten to breathe. He sucked in a long, shuddering breath. 'We did it,' he told Dad.

Curtis dragged hand over his face. 'I'm done in. Get me a cold beer, will you, son?'

Jay walked zombie-like into the kitchen. He'd lost all sense of time. He thought it was night. But when he looked out Curtis's window, at his collection of scrapyard cars, they glowed red and gold. The sun was only just setting.

He realized he was ravenous. He tipped half a packet of cheese crackers into his mouth, crunched them, then wolfed down the rest.

He brought the beer back to Curtis. Cracked the can open, helpfully, before he handed it over.

'Is she gonna die?' he asked Curtis, willing him to say, 'No.'

Curtis took a swig of beer, glanced over at Dusk. She was sleeping, breathing easier. Her skin was pink now, instead of bluish-grey.

'I don't think so,' said Curtis. 'Think she'll be all right. But that's powerful poison that old bitch uses. Lucky Dusk only got a trace of it. Else her heart would've stopped quick as that.' Curtis clicked his fingers. Jay shuddered.

Jay sat down, opposite his dad. Tried to make eye contact with him, like he had with Dusk by the lily pond. But Curtis's eyes slipped away.

Jay persisted. He knew Dad's habit of putting things off, making excuses. But this time Jay wasn't going to let Dad escape. 'How did you know her name?' he asked Curtis, straight out. 'Why didn't you want to take her to a hospital? Tell me, Dad.'

Curtis squirmed uneasily in his creaky chair. He could see it was confession time.

'You remember when I worked at SERU?'

Jay nodded.

'Well, I saw her there. I wasn't supposed to but I sneaked into the lab where they kept her. She was an experiment.'

Jay said, bewildered, 'What you talking about?'

'They made her in a test tube in a laboratory,' said Curtis. 'Don't know where they got the eggs and sperm. But they used a surrogate mother, somebody local. I don't

153

know much about that part of it, just what I learned from a computer disk. That all happened way before I got the job. And it wasn't my business to know anyway, I was just a lab assistant. Anyhow, what I do know is that they wanted to see if humans could have perfect night vision like hawks. So they put hawk genes into her embryo.'

'You're kidding me!' Jay blurted out.

His mind felt blown apart by this information. It was seconds before he could even begin to take it in. But then he saw Curtis wasn't kidding. And when he thought about it, it all fitted together. How she looked, how she hunted, what she ate.

'I saw her eat a rat,' said Jay. 'I saw her kill one.'

So she learned to feed herself, did she? thought Curtis. He'd always known Dusk was smarter than the scientists supposed. He said to Jay, 'Well, she was just doing what hawks do.'

'But she's human!' protested Jay. 'She don't think she is, but she's got human feelings just like us. What about . . .' His words tumbled over each other; he wanted to ask a million questions.

'Course she's human.' Curtis's slow, drawling voice cut through Jay's impatience. 'Only it suited the military not to treat her like that. They treated her like a wild animal. But if they knew she was alive –'

'What? What if they knew?' said Jay.

'That's why we couldn't take her to no doctor. The military would get to hear about it, for sure. They'd take her back. She's their property. We can't trust no one. The military would take her back – then pay a fortune to

154

whoever found her, to hush it all up. What they did to her, it'd cause a scandal if it leaked out.'

'So what we gonna do with her, Dad?' asked Jay.

Curtis frowned. He couldn't see any future for Dusk. Not with them anyway. He felt guilty about it but he knew they couldn't handle her, that she'd need specialist care.

But he didn't want to let Jay down. Not like all the other times. He could see that, at the moment, Jay was looking to him for solutions, depending on him. Even feeling grateful to him. Because he'd caught Dusk as she fell, taken control when she was sick. It was a good feeling, to have his own son not look at him with contempt.

'Look,' said Curtis, his mind drifting away to other things he felt guilty about. 'I know my life's a mess. I know I've let people down. And your Ma, well, being religious and all, she was always too good for me but . . .'

Jay shook his head impatiently. He wasn't interested in all that now. Besides, he'd heard it all before. But he pretended to listen. Curtis deserved not to be interrupted. He'd been a hero today.

While Curtis was rambling on, Jay looked down at his fingers. The skin between them was crusty with scabs, where the burns were healing over. He stared at them as if the hands belonged to someone else. To a kid he didn't know. Had he really made those? He must have been crazy, hurting himself like that.

'Look, Dad, what we gonna do with Dusk?' asked Jay again, when Curtis stopped talking to swallow some beer.

155

'I don't know,' said Curtis, dragging his mind back to the main problem. He told himself, *Look, you gotta stop pretending she can stay with us. Just break it to the boy. But gently.*

'Trouble is,' he began, 'she can't be socialized –'

'You're not saying she'd be better off back with them?' said Jay, horrified.

'No, no,' said Curtis. 'Just calm down a second. I'm just saying that, well, it's a real headache thinking what to do with her. We don't want to keep her shut up like she was before.'

'No way!' said Jay clenching his fists furiously.

'But we can't let no one see her. Not till we've decided what to do. Case they go running to the military. Or the press.'

'No press,' agreed Jay. 'She'd be treated like a freak show.'

Curtis nodded, sadly. 'I know. She just don't fit in anywhere.'

'So why can't she live here with us?' demanded Jay.

Curtis pretended he hadn't heard the question. He thought, *The boy's had a really rough time. He's worn out. He'll see sense in the morning.*

He took another swig of beer. Looked at Dusk sleeping. 'So she's been living in Prospect all this time?' Curtis shook his head in admiration. 'I always knew she was a fighter. But I never thought she could survive that long on her own.'

'You don't know the half of it, Dad,' said Jay. 'There were rats, like hundreds of them. And these dogs. I got bit.

156

By the way, you got any antiseptic? You should put some on your neck too.'

But Curtis wasn't listening. He was thinking, *Poor little freak*. Dusk's wilderness had burned down. She was back in civilization now, where survival was going to be a whole lot harder.

'And they killed my hound dog,' Jay was saying.

That made Curtis pay attention. 'What? The one you gave the collar to?' Curtis was sorry about that. 'He was a good dog,' he said.

Jay nodded. His head sank into his hands. It was all too much, the last thirty-six hours. Emotions were crashing over him in waves. He didn't want Dad to see he was crying, helplessly, like a baby.

Curtis dragged himself out of the chair, put a hand on Jay's shoulder. 'Go to bed, son,' he said. 'You're just worn out. I'll watch Dusk. Things'll look better tomorrow.'

Jay nodded, sniffed, wiped his streaming nose with the back of his hand, got up. He nodded at Curtis and smiled. Tonight he'd seen his dad in a new light. Sides of Curtis Ma had never told him about. Curtis had been strong, reliable, known what to do.

'Dad,' Jay mumbled, swaying on his feet, 'you did really good today. I mean, you were a . . .'

'Go to bed, son,' repeated Curtis.

Jay staggered off. He didn't even get into bed. Just collapsed on top of it, sprawled like a starfish. He fell instantly into a dreamless sleep.

15

Jud, jud, jud, jud, jud.

In his sleep, Jay heard a noise. He groaned, ignored it, turned over.

Jud, jud, jud, jud.

It didn't go away. He shook himself awake. Staggered over to the window. *What's that racket?* he thought. *Waking me up!*

It was really loud, right above the house. The trees were blowing about as if a hurricane had hit them.

Curtis came running into the bedroom. 'It's a military 'copter!' he said.

Jud, jud, jud. The noise was fainter. Moving away.

'They've gone,' said Jay, relieved. 'How's Dusk?'

'She's OK,' said Curtis hurriedly. 'But, look Jay. You don't understand. I think they know about Dusk. If they do, they'll be back. With ground troops. They'll search the woods. They won't give up.'

'How?' shouted Jay. 'How do they know about her?' A dreadful suspicion burst into his brain. Left him reeling. He should have known – Curtis being a hero was too good to be true.

'Who knew about her?' he raved at Curtis. 'Just you and me! You told them, didn't you? You called them, when I was asleep. You said last night, they'd pay money –'

'What do you think I am?' Curtis yelled, horrified. He didn't often raise his voice to Jay but this time he was so shocked he couldn't help himself. 'I can't believe you just said that! Haven't you got any faith at all in me, boy? Don't you even suggest that! That I'd . . .' He shook his head, too hurt to carry on.

Jay yelled back, 'Yeah, yeah, give me your usual excuses! How it wasn't your fault!'

Curtis lifted his hand. He had never hit Jay. He left the discipline to his mother. But he was so wounded, so outraged, he couldn't control himself. Just when he thought he and Jay were getting on better!

Then he thought, *What am I doing?* He let his hand drop, struggled to keep his voice steady. 'Look, I never called the military. I thought she couldn't stay here, I can't deny that. But I'd never hand her back to them!'

Jay opened his mouth to yell. 'You –!'

'Look, we ain't got time to quarrel,' Curtis butted in. 'We've got to get Dusk out of here.'

Jay didn't believe him. Curtis had let him down too much in the past. He could barely bring himself to speak to him, he felt so betrayed, disgusted. Jay knew his dad was a loser. But he hadn't thought he'd sink to this, selling Dusk back to the military for money.

'No!' he said to Curtis, furiously. 'I don't trust you. Me and Dusk are going alone. We don't want you with us.'

'Don't be stupid! You're not talking sense!'

159

But Curtis hadn't reckoned on the fierce loyalty Jay felt to Dusk. After they'd faced death together, fought for their lives in Prospect.

Jay pushed his dad aside, ran into the living room. Dusk was still asleep, her white-blonde hair tangled on the pillow. Her orange eyes shot open, instantly alert, on the defensive.

'Dusk, we got to go,' said Jay, frantically. He didn't look at Curtis. He couldn't. It was just him and Dusk now. Curtis didn't exist.

But Dusk had seen Curtis. She wasn't on the edge of coma, like she had been yesterday. Today she recognized him, instantly. She was confused, scrambled out of bed, a sheet still tangled round her. She tripped, screeched, clawed her hands to defend herself.

'See! She don't like you either!' shouted Jay. 'Just back off. Leave us alone!'

How am I going to deal with this? thought Curtis. He couldn't waste time trying to argue. The only thing that mattered was to get Dusk out of here.

What he suggested was out of sheer desperation.

'Here!' He kept well away from them both. Jay was standing beside Dusk now, trying to soothe her. Curtis fumbled in his pocket, slid car keys across the floor, some money. He couldn't think what else to do. Dusk didn't seem to want him near her. And somebody had to stay behind to throw the military off the trail.

'Take the truck,' he said to Jay. 'They'll be looking for the four-by-four. I'll stay here. There's something I've got to do. You take Dusk to Otter Lake; you remember where

160

that is? It's fifty miles north – where we used to go to fish. Then call me. We'll meet up there. Wait a minute.'

Careful not to make any sudden moves that might alarm Dusk, he skimmed his mobile across the floor to Jay.

'Call me on the house phone. If I don't answer, keep trying until you get me.'

'Come on,' said Jay to Dusk. 'We're leaving.'

'Keep to the back roads,' said Curtis. 'Don't let anyone see her.'

Dusk shrank back, even from Jay. Her mind was in turmoil, her familiar world snatched away. She had no idea how to function in this new one. The poison was mostly gone from her system. But she still felt weak as a newborn lamb, unable to defend herself.

Frantically, Jay tried to think himself into her mind. What could he say to persuade her?

'Dusk,' he said. 'Listen. Right?'

Dusk stared at him, her hands clawing at her arms convulsively, but not yet breaking the flesh. At the same time she had her eyes on Curtis. But he'd backed away into the shadows of the bedroom. He was scrabbling in drawers looking for something he thought she'd like.

Jay could see Dusk was distracted. 'Listen to me,' he begged again. 'I'm going to tell you something good. Remember Prospect, where you lived? Well, we'll find another Prospect. I promise. I'm gonna take you there. Now. Right now.'

Did she believe him? He fixed his eyes on hers, like he had that time by the lily pond when Wolf was prowling

161

round, breathing down their necks, his eyes wild and blood-flecked.

'Don't look at Curtis,' he said. 'Look at me.'

And something strange happened, even in the confusion and chaos of the present moment. Jay didn't expect it – it was mystical. Before, he didn't like it when his mind got mystical. But now he treasured it.

Because for a few seconds, as their eyes locked, it seemed that he and Dusk were in a protective bubble. That they had their own personal defence shield. Wolves could be prowling outside, the military were searching, Curtis could betray them. But none of that mattered. He and Dusk were safe, beyond their reach. Nothing could harm them.

But another voice broke the spell. 'Dusk, I got a present for you.'

Jay glowered at Curtis, his eyes full of bitterness.

'I been keeping it all this time,' said Curtis, holding out the plastic hair slide with the fake glass rubies. 'Just in case. Look, it's pretty.'

Dusk followed the glitter. Stretched out her hand to take the hair slide. Jay couldn't believe it. She was smiling at Curtis, as if she trusted him. Didn't she know what he was like?

'Don't listen to him,' said Jay. 'Don't take his cheesy present!'

He snatched the money, the mobile and the truck keys off the floor. His eyes on Curtis now, he backed to the door.

'Come on,' said Jay. 'We don't need him.'

There was so much contempt in his voice that Curtis cried out, 'Jay, believe me, I didn't tell them.' He was still holding out the slide for Dusk.

But Dusk, confused again, had backed off. She moved closer to Jay.

'You know who I am, don't you, Dusk?' coaxed Curtis. 'I saved you from the fire. I wouldn't hurt you.'

But Jay looked at him with such hatred that Curtis had to turn away, the hair slide dangling uselessly from his hand.

'I'll spin the military some story,' he mumbled. 'Put 'em off the scent.'

But Jay was already on his way out of the door.

Curtis heard the truck start up. He shook his head, sighing. Dragged his hand down over his face. *What a mess,'* he thought. *What an almighty mess.*

He waited until the truck's engine died away. Then hurried out into the yard. He started up the four-by-four, spun the wheels on the gravel and shot off up the dirt track. He was heading for Mrs Olafsen's.

The four-by-four screeched to a stop. She was feeding her doves. They were fluttering around her like big, white butterflies. Curtis jumped out, ran heavily towards her house. There was a new crucified hawk on her home-made gibbet. Curtis didn't even glance at it.

He was breathing hard. 'You witch,' he said to her. 'What did you tell them? Always snooping around, spying. Why don't you mind your own damn business. 'Stead of sticking your nose into everybody else's!'

163

'Why, Curtis,' said Mrs Olafsen, frowning, 'what's got you so worked up?'

'I ain't got time to play games,' said Curtis. 'I know she wasn't your true biological daughter. But you carried her for nine months, gave birth to her. Didn't you feel nothing for her?'

Mrs Olafsen's face grew ugly. But she shook her head stubbornly. 'I don't know what you're talking about.'

'Don't bother trying to deny it,' said Curtis. 'I know it was you. Those scientists shouldn't leave their computer disks lying around for anyone to look at.'

Mrs Olafsen was quiet for a few seconds. Then she shuddered. 'The little monster. I was glad when they took her away. She weren't nothing to me.'

'Except a whole heap of money,' yelled Curtis into her face. 'How much did they pay you? How much are they still paying you to keep quiet?'

But Mrs Olafsen didn't want to talk about that.

'Yeah,' said Curtis. 'That's right. Pretend none of it happened.' He could feel the veins in his forehead bulging. His blood pressure soaring. *Calm down*, he ordered himself. Having a heart attack wasn't going to help Dusk and Jay.

'Listen,' he said to her, fighting to keep his voice steady. 'You'd better change your story. Say you were a silly woman. Say you never saw what you thought you saw.'

'They won't believe me,' said Mrs Olafsen.

'Make 'em believe you! Say you were drunk!'

'I can't do that,' said Mrs Olafsen. 'I never touch a drop and everyone around here knows it. Anyway, you got no right to keep her. She's better off with the military. It's not right to let something like her loose, among decent, civilized folks. She should be kept where no one can see her.'

Curtis gritted his teeth. Tried to control his temper. The doves cooed and fluttered round his head. He waved his arms to shoo them off.

'Listen, you bitch. She died. Right? Died because of your poisoned bait. Don't suppose you'll be sad about that. But if you don't change your story I'm going to tell the press all about you. Tell the TV stations. You'll be charged with murder. Of your own daughter.'

'She weren't no blood relation to me! She weren't even human!'

'She's as human as you or me! More human than you, that's for sure! And you cooperated in criminal experiments. For money. You'll spend the rest of your life in jail.'

Mrs Olafsen looked thoughtful. 'What would my doves do without me?' she said.

'Hawks'll get 'em,' said Curtis.

That, more than any other argument, decided Mrs Olafsen. 'What do you want me to do?' she asked Curtis, tight-lipped.

'Call the military. I mean, *now*. I don't care what you tell 'em. But make them believe that you made a mistake. That you never saw Dusk at all. That it was just my son, Jay, you saw with me. No one else.'

'I picked up a baseball cap,' said Mrs Olafsen. 'Black, some silver nonsense on it. You left it behind.'

'Good,' said Curtis. 'That's Jay's. Now show 'em that. And tell 'em you ain't sure any more about what you saw.'

Curtis drove back home like a boy racer, trailing dust clouds behind him. He knew that whatever Mrs Olafsen told them, they would still come to him to check out her story. He sat on his front porch to wait for them. His heart was racing, his mouth dry. He took a swig of beer. When they came, he would have to give the performance of his life.

Jay drove north to Otter Lake. He'd never driven the truck before. It took him a while to get used to it. Dusk was in the front seat beside him. He wished Dusk had the cap. He wondered what had happened to it. She could have pulled it down low to disguise herself. But it was remote country up here. They only saw one other vehicle, a lorry carrying logs. When it passed, Jay made Dusk duck down.

Dusk screeched suddenly and stuck her head out the open window. Harsh, wild cries were coming from way above them. High up, drifting lazily on the thermals, was a lone hawk.

Dusk called to it, shrill excited cries. It swooped away. Her eyes yearned after it. Her skinny elbows flapped. Jay's head shot round, alarmed.

'You can't fly,' he reminded her, his eyes back on the road. 'You won't try that again, will you? You're human, like me.'

Dusk didn't answer. Her third eyelids slid across her eyes, then back.

Jay glanced at her. He couldn't tell what she was thinking. Had she admitted to herself yet that she was only human? That she had human limitations?

166

'You all right?' he asked her. She was very silent, beside him, her head drooping on her chest. Not even making hawk noises. He was suddenly scared about what was going on in her head. Scared that if he stopped, let her out, she'd run away from him, into the woods.

'Look,' he said awkwardly. 'We'll find somewhere. I promise. We'll go further north – where there are no people.'

Jay had only a hazy idea what was up there. He'd heard there was still virgin forest, some of it unmapped. 'That's where we'll go,' he said to Dusk. 'Further.'

Two days ago he'd thought where Curtis lived was the end of the world.

'It'll be better than Prospect,' added Jay. 'Without the rats. Or those dogs. Or people.'

Dusk didn't seem to be listening. But she lifted her head. Her eyes glittered. Instinctively she shot her hand out the truck window, snatched a passing dragonfly. Crammed it, still fluttering, into her mouth.

Jay said, 'You're OK again!'

He gazed ahead at the road. It felt like it was him and Dusk against the world. Just the two of them.

Who else is there to trust? he thought.

Dad had betrayed Dusk. Maybe. He was having second thoughts about that. Maybe he'd been too quick to jump to conclusions. *But, who else could it be?* he argued with himself. And Ma? Ma couldn't deal with this. She'd say, 'Trust in Jesus and everything will be all right.'

Jay thought, *I don't trust no one. Only us.*

*

Curtis was having a beer to calm his nerves. The military had been and gone. There were three of them. But he thought he'd done OK. They'd left thinking he was a shambling, drunken wreck. They'd searched the place – good job he'd destroyed that computer disk long ago. They'd given up trying to get any sense out of him.

'This is getting us nowhere,' said the young guy in charge, clean-cut and handsome in his crisp military uniform. He'd looked at Curtis in disgust. Curtis knew what he was thinking. *Drunken slob*, when Curtis was more sober than he'd been for years.

'You hear anything, you let us know. Right?'

They'd stamped off in their big shiny boots. Driven away in their jeep.

Curtis had given a long, long sigh of relief. He'd never sweated so much in his life.

He went around his house, packing the stuff they'd need; food, clothes. He wasn't planning to come back. He might have put the military off for a while. But he didn't think they'd give up.

Then he sat by the phone, waiting for Jay to ring. Now he could tell him, for sure, who had betrayed Dusk to the military. *He didn't really think it was me, did he?* thought Curtis. That still hurt him. He hadn't thought Jay's opinion of him was that low.

The other thing he wanted to tell him was: 'I'm with you, boy. You and me, we'll look after Dusk. Keep her safe. Make her happy. We'll do whatever it takes.'

Curtis waited and waited. The phone didn't ring.

*

Jay stopped the truck by the lake. There was no one around. Not even anyone out in a fishing boat. It was beautiful, so quiet and peaceful. The trees fringing it were a soft green blur, the water a shimmering silver disc.

Dusk had been sleeping most of the way. Now she was awake, looking around, feeling stronger, her orange eyes alert, on full beam. She screeched in excitement. What had she seen? Probably a mouse in the grass.

'If I let you out, you won't run, will you?' asked Jay anxiously. He wanted her to be with him, in his new future. He couldn't imagine it without her.

'Dusk hungry,' said Dusk.

He got out with her. She crouched in the cool green grass, froze for a second, pounced.

'Hey, you caught a lizard!' said Jay.

He was hungry too. He crammed some blueberries off a bush into his mouth, stooped down to scoop some water from the lake, lapped it out of his cupped hands.

Dusk watched him. Affectionate but curious. As if he was a different species.

Jay took his dad's mobile out the pocket of his shorts. He was supposed to call Curtis. Dad would join them here. That had been the arrangement.

But he'd already decided he wasn't going to call. For a few seconds he felt overwhelmed by despair and self pity. He couldn't trust Curtis, couldn't trust anyone. The sense of aloneness swamped him.

He shook himself, like a dog. 'It's just us two,' he told Dusk. It felt kind of romantic to say that. But Jay was already thinking, *It's impossible.*

Could they stay one step ahead of the military? Could they find somewhere Dusk could hide away from people? Was there any place like that left on the planet?

He had to have faith there was.

We'll find it, he thought, scowling in determination. And when they found it, what then? She could survive in the wilderness. Could he? Maybe he'd have to leave her there.

No, he thought fiercely. *I'm not gonna do that. She'll teach me.*

But there were more immediate problems. Soon their money would run out. He knew he'd have to go into a town soon, to get more gas and other supplies. What about cigarettes? He hadn't had one for two days. Hadn't thought about them. Well, not all that much anyway. But he'd sure like one now.

If things got really bad, if they needed help, more money, he might have to phone Curtis.

Maybe he was telling the truth, Jay tried to persuade himself. *Maybe he didn't tell the military.* He wanted so much to believe it.

But not yet. He wouldn't phone Curtis yet, Jay decided, putting the mobile back in his pocket. And if his dad came looking, he wouldn't find them. The lake was beautiful. It was tempting to stay here. But it wasn't far enough. They were moving on.

Moving on. Jay liked the sound of that. He started smiling, he just couldn't help himself. He forgot all his fears. 'Chill out,' he ordered himself.

He suddenly felt reborn, as if he'd sloughed off his old

life like a snake skin. As if he had a glittering, fresh new one. Little Shane seemed irrelevant. The pain game, who needed it?

Have to call Ma though, a little voice prodded him at the back of his mind. *She'll be worrying. Have to call her some time.*

Some time. But not yet. Not yet. He didn't want to think about all that stuff now. It reminded him too much of the old Jay. The Jay he never wanted to go back to. It felt to him that, after thirty-six hours in Prospect, he was a different person. Different even to what he was before he got beat up. But he liked this Jay better. He was scared that if he went back to his old life, he'd lose him.

He was driving now, with Dusk beside him. Suddenly he laughed out loud at the craziness of life, put his foot down, speeded up. He felt a leap in his heart, was happier than he'd ever been before. He was suddenly sure things would work out.

It's now that matters, he told himself, like he'd told Dusk by the lily pond.

Birds of prey were common up here. There was another one, over the trees. Jay slowed down.

And another one! A hawk streaking in from the north, flying strongly. It had something, a gift of food, dangling from its talons.

'Lizard,' Dusk told Jay. He nodded, as if he had her vision.

But she could see much more than Jay could – each individual barb on its feathers, each scale on its feet. The glittering brightness of its eyes.

171

The hawk passed the gift to its mate. They locked feet, began a fantastic twirling dance until, just above the trees, they broke apart, swooped away together.

Dusk watched them fly away. Her heart ached. Jay glanced at her, uneasily. Did she feel the same sense of freedom he did? He wanted her to.

But Dusk had her own dreams of freedom. That time she'd crashed to the earth – she was in denial; she'd cancelled it from her mind. Dusk had faith again. Surely she couldn't be only human? She had a picture in her head. Dusk saw herself, up there, with the hawks. Soaring, drifting lazily. She could even feel warm air currents, cradling her body . . .

'I am Dusk,' she murmured to herself, smiling.

Jay glanced at her again. She looked happy now. Happy to be with him. That was just how he wanted it to be.

Jay speeded up again.

The truck headed north, moving fast, following the hawks.